AS TOLD BY THINGS

AS TOLD BY THINGS

EDITED BY E.D.E. Bell

Atthis Arts, LLC

AS TOLD BY THINGS

Published by Atthis Arts, LLC
Detroit, Michigan
atthisarts.com

ISBN 978-1-945009-14-3

Library of Congress Control Number: 2018905235

Contents

Preface

Working on this collection has been a lot of fun.

While I was thinking of anthology ideas, I mused that my favorite collections are not just those with a common theme and engaging stories, but those where, as a reader, I'm excited for each new story—excited to discover what angle different authors will take on a concept that is open for broad interpretation.

I settled on an idea that I found interesting to think about and one I kept returning to: stories from the perspective of objects. There was some concern that it was too ambitious for an anthology call—especially the first from a small press—but I'm glad I stuck with it, because the stories that we received are . . . wonderful.

I was especially excited to create a multi-genre collection, tied together by both the theme as well as the requested tone of light, witty, and charming. I think it worked! Some stories are silly, some are sexy, some are inspiring—each is quite different. I stayed away from darker or more serious topics, because I wanted to provide readers an escape, and offer something that is, well, fun!

The stories are on the short side. You can read the collection all at once, like an art exhibit, or you can take in a story here or there, in line, on the bus, or at home for a break.

My gratitude goes out to all the talented authors who submitted stories; each of their love, effort, and artistry is greatly appreciated.

As a small press and in support of many talented indie authors, reviews are very important to us. If you enjoy the collection, I'd appreciate you taking your time to leave a rating and review on your preferred apps and sites. If you're not sure what to say, just say that you enjoyed it.

Now, what stories do objects have to tell?

Cheers,
E.D.E. Bell
June 2018

Start Again

By Alanna McFall

It first came to know glass walls. The earliest stirrings of awareness occurred when it was bubbling away and cradled by smooth surfaces, hard material below and around it and air above. Later it learned that these planes were a Jar, and far above it was a Lid. Slightly open to let the air in, the Lid did not matter much until it was moved to make way for the Spoon.

The Spoon was the second thing it became aware of, reaching down toward it and parting it. Sections of it were dragged away, stolen through the Lid to go someplace else, but there was no pain. It was one size, and then by the grace of the Spoon it became lesser, but there was no reason to mourn. The Spoon also brought life with it, sprinkled down from the sky and added to it. The Spoon dragged through its mass and mixed the life, the wet Food, in until the new became part of the whole. The life felt different from what already made up itself, but good, filling. Later it would hear the words that captured the life. Flour. Water. Its own name was said one day and it thought it was fitting: Starter. It was only just starting to be aware, starting to be everything, so that was a good name. Starter, content and warm in its Jar, fed by a Spoon bringing Flour and Water. Its life felt good. It felt good to have life.

Yeast is what they called the bubbling up inside. "I think we're getting some real yeast in there, Babe," Hon said. It took Starter a long time to process out the words and the meanings, but it had all the time it needed. The only thing it had to do was grow and think.

Hon, also known as Honey, was the one who fed it by way of the Spoon. When Starter came to cast its awareness through the

Jar and see the places beyond, it realized that it could see Hon approaching with the mix of life in its own container. Hon was the bringer of food and warmth and the pleasant disruption of the Spoon. As much as there could be fondness, as much as Starter could feel pleasant emotions toward something that had brought it pleasant emotions, it liked Hon. Hon was good to it.

Babe was a more complicated situation. Babe separated and took and used. Hon would split its body and take part of it away for Babe to use. When it focused on life outside of the Jar, it could sometimes see what had happened to the parts of it that were removed. They were occasionally set near the Jar, rigid and browned pieces that had been life. They had been stretched and pressed and subjected to heat and there was not life in them anymore. But the warmth that radiated off the mounds made them difficult to hate. In the smell rolling out from that heat, Starter could tell that these things were a part of it, removed and gone off to do something else. Bread, the mounds were called. If there was a point to all of this, it seemed to be Bread. Hon tended to Starter and Babe made Bread and the whole of Starter's world made sense.

And so it was, when Starter came to awareness and grew and ate and grew and grew more. There was the Jar and the Spoon and Flour and Water and the Lid, and far above it were Hon and Babe. More things surrounded the Jar in the world that was its home, its kitchen, but they did not impact its life and did not matter, and the things that did matter stayed. Things changed from day to day, just as Starter developed and was separated and replaced, but it all came back and grew in perfect equilibrium.

Until Babe was gone.

Hon and Babe had been speaking loudly, disrupting the quiet of the world, and using strange words at each other for a long time by then—many, many rounds of feeding and baking. Through the open space below Lid, Starter could hear them shouting.

"Well, if you like her so much, why aren't you with her?"

"She's not even gay; stop being so paranoid!"

Bread did not tend to be made on days with loud words, and the pieces taken from Starter would disappear to parts unknown. There had to be calm in the world for Bread, and as strange of a creation as it was, Starter missed its warmth when there was none. As the loud days increased in number, Hon discarded more and more Starter and there was no Bread. But when the days grew quieter again, the creation of Bread did not resume. The kitchen was cold, Babe and Hon were quiet, and all Starter could do was bubble and grow, as it always had.

For a few days, no Flour or Water were brought to it. That was normal, that was the way of things, until it stretched out for a few more days. Then a few more. Starter's thoughts started to slow and its world started to dim. When the Spoon came back, accompanied by Hon's voice, it could barely comprehend what was happening.

It was divided once more and replenished with Flour and Water, but strange words in a hushed tone drifted into its hazy mind.

"Here, Ba—here. You should take this. You're the one who could use it the most."

" . . . I'll take half."

"No, really, you can have—"

"I don't think either of us is going to be baking anytime soon; it'll just get thrown away. Now we each have our own. To . . . to remember."

"Babe—"

"I have to go."

That was the last Starter heard of Babe's voice. The Lid was put back on, tighter than usual, and the sounds of the outside world were dulled. Starter took in its Flour and Water and replenished its life, but could not hear what went on around it.

The world was colder and quieter and not filled with heat and voices. For many feeding cycles, there was no Bread set next to the Jar, though half of Starter was always taken and discarded. Its mind grew deeper and more aware, but it began to wonder if Bread had been a dream. After so long, where was the proof that it had ever been there to begin with? Feeding cycles passed. Hon was still there and continued to open the Jar and feed it, but Hon's voice was almost as absent as Babe's. Beyond the lack of Bread, there were no other cooking smells or heat, the strange things that had filled the kitchen before and confused Starter. There was just cold. Occasional hot things came wrapped in cardboard or paper, but nothing was created. Starter's world had stopped being one of creation and production, beyond the constant growth that it produced. It grew with no purpose, growth for the sake of growth.

"I should just throw you out," Hon muttered to it one day. "I'm only wasting flour."

Starter's Jar was picked up and opened a half-dozen times over the next few days, dangled over a can where Hon and Babe had put things they did not want. But Hon always paused and replaced the lid eventually. Perhaps this was a new pattern of Starter's life, though it did not seem to be one with a purpose.

When its Jar was opened again, Starter expected the same treatment and was shocked to feel its home actually tilt and turn, its body pulled out of the only home it had ever known. Was this how all the other pieces had felt when they were taken away? Was this what being turned into Bread was? Its life had been so comfortable and warm and nourished that it was a shock to feel fear. It was a shock to feel cold.

Starter was stretched and spread over a wider surface than it had ever known before. Perhaps this was the path to becoming Bread, it thought. Perhaps this was normal and right and heat would be coming soon. Starter held onto this hope long into the persisting cold.

A slow drying followed, and brought with it a gradual slowing of Starter's thoughts. Time passed with it spread out in the air, far longer than it had ever felt air breezing in through the open lid of the Jar. It was not dying, it thought; there was no undoing of the Life that had been bubbling inside it for so long, but there was no more growth. No more Life came, no Flour nor Water, and it could not even muster the thoughts to mourn their absence. Everything was missing, which soon came to include the very awareness that there was something missing. The world stayed cold, Hon did not touch it or feed it, and all was cold and dry. Its thoughts slowed . . . and slowed . . . and slowed.

Hard. Brittle. It worked up maybe one thought a day, a slow observation that Hon barely looked at it any more, or that the light felt warm, but also seemed to make it drier. Its body splintered in strange ways, sharp edges when it had only known soft liquid curves. There was nothing soft about its reality now. The world was flat. Things existed above and around it, but the breadth of its experience was flat. And then, broken.

Pieces. Being broken. This was nothing like the splitting that Hon had done before, this was not part of it going off to be made into Bread, this was a split, a series of splits through its very core. It was picked and scooped by fingers that were not gentle, by motions that were not mixing, but breaking. One piece, another piece, cracked and taken, in body and in mind. Its mind was splitting too, each piece a separate slow thought being taken away from the whole. If there even was a whole anymore, or just all pieces. There was a vague awareness of its parts being put in another container, another home, but this one was different, colder than the home it had always known. And far above it, a lid shut tight. No warmth, no air. And in this way, slowly, slowly over time, Starter stopped. It did not die, it was not gone. It was stopped.

If asked, it could not tell how much time went by in the container so unlike its home. On occasion it was aware of light. Or of dark. But not with any sort of continuity or cycle. Most of the time there was only cold. Cold and still.

For a very long time.

Cold.

Still.

Stopped.

. . .

. . .

. . .

Until one day . . .

"Okay, let's see if there's anything left in you."

Hon's voice was there for a moment, then gone. For more time, there was nothing. Then one day, there was something. There was a start. In a soup of Flour and Water, there was a start.

Several days later, there was Starter. Awareness slowly curled back into it with each stir, Air and Flour coming into it and reawakening long sleeping things. It had slept in dryness, and through Water it was coming back into the world. Water and Flour softened and recombined broken pieces and broken thoughts. It was one body; it was one mind. It was returned to its Jar, and in those moments of transition, it could feel how warm the world outside was. For the first time since Babe had gone, the world had returned to warmth. Starter flourished in the new attention and care. Its fondness for Hon slowly woke up along with the Yeast. And when the time came and the life was bubbling and moving inside it, Hon made Bread.

Hon took half of Starter and used it to make a warm, full-grown pile of Bread that smelled familiar, made of Starter's body and a kin in its flesh. Once more, this was a place where Bread was made.

Perhaps the production of Bread was what brought more Bread into Starter's world, Bread that was even more different but still rang true with a familiar lineage. For one day, Hon brought a loaf of Bread from further outside, from out past the kitchen, and it was wrapped in paper and still warm. And from the smell, Starter got an inkling of where it was from. A common root that had diverged, developed off in its own direction, but still smelled like home.

"Not like I need bread . . . " Hon muttered, one hand on the loaf and one on Starter's Jar. "But that was nice of her."

The Bread was from Babe's hands, from what had once been Starter until it became its own creature, but it looked at home in Hon's arms, in Hon's kitchen. It had been brought home.

It was a start.

⊹

Alanna McFall is a writer and actor originally from Minnesota. She has published with Mad Scientist Journal, Escape Pod, Alliteration Ink, and many more. She is a member of the Monday Night PlayGround Writer's Pool in San Francisco for the 2017-2018 season, and has been happy to present two pieces for staged readings with the Writer's Pool. In addition to writing, she works as Publicity Manager for Kinetic Arts Center, a circus theater in Oakland.

The Lady at the Bar

By B.C. Kalis

I remember the first time I saw her. She walked through the door, a small glint of relief in her tired eyes. A few strands of her hair had escaped her updo and hung down over her face. She still had her uniform on from work: a server's apron with pens lining the hem and a few receipts poking out from one of the pockets. A name tag peeked out from under her coat. She stood in the doorway for a moment, tucking her hair back behind her ear. She didn't notice me at first. She was looking at the bartender behind me. She gave a small smile—a friendly smile, a smile that seemed to say *everything is okay now that I'm here.*

As she began making her way to the bar, she removed her apron and rolled it into a bundle, which she tied up and stuffed into one of her coat pockets. She slipped the coat from her shoulders, and the tension seemed to release from her with every step as she got closer. She draped her coat over the back of a bar chair, closed her eyes, tilted her head back and let out a small sigh. The bartender—who embodied bartender perfection: white coat, black bowtie, well-greased pompadour, and a million-dollar smile—put one elbow on the oak bar and leaned toward her and asked with the smoothness of a crooner, "What'll it be, kid?"

Her eyes opened and her head straightened, and she had the cutest smirk on her face as she sat down next to me and said, "The usual, my friend." I'd felt a chill run through me as she approached, and I was frozen stiff as she sat down next to me. But when she looked at me—when she looked at me and smiled—it was almost too much. Not the same friendly smile she gave the bartender, but the "I want you" smile. The type that doesn't just make you feel needed, but desired. Everything started to melt; pure light began to build inside of me, expanding into every part of my being, burning away every chill and all the coldness I had just experienced.

I had never felt this way before. Her eyes! Her eyes were the most beautiful things I had ever seen. They were green, sea green, and like the ocean I was lost in them, drifting in a sea I had no intention of returning from. They were the type of eyes that let you know she knew everything you were thinking, that she knew every one of your secrets, and all the secrets to the universe for that matter, but still wanted you to tell her what she wanted to hear.

She kept shifting back and forth between looking at me with adoration and looking at the bartender with courtesy. When her eyes were trained on me, there was a spark of desire in them, and her smile grew, and she would sometimes bite her bottom lip. When she pulled her gaze back to the man behind the bar, her eyes would drop and her smile would turn to a more embarrassed one, as though she'd been caught doing something she ought not be doing. She would regain her composure and look up at the bartender and continue their conversation, but her eyes would still glance over at me every few seconds. During one of the moments she was talking to the tender, describing a customer who had made her already long day longer, she slid her hand around my side and pulled me close to her, never once saying a word to me, just pulling me in and holding me close. Her hand was warm, and while her touch was soft, it was also strong. There was no hesitation in her choice or her actions, and there was no resistance in mine.

The bartender gave her a nod and a wink, turned his back to us, and began walking to the far side of the bar, whistling a soft tune and polishing a rocks glass. I had been desiring, and dreading, the moment when I would be left alone with her.

She looked at me and smiled, and her pull increased slowly, drawing me even closer. If I had to trade every perfect sunrise, sunset, full moon, shining star, and sparkling snowflake this world had ever seen, just to have that smile one more time, I wouldn't think twice about it. Without hesitation, she grabbed me, pulled me close. Her eyes closed, she pressed her lips to mine, and drained my spirit. She quickly pulled away. Her eyes were still closed, her complete appearance relaxed, as if she had finally found what she was looking for—complete satisfaction. She had stolen everything from inside me, and if I had more, I would have given it to her.

She smirked, wiped her lips, pushed me back against the hard oak bar, which was a complete contrast to her soft embrace, and stood up. I didn't think it possible for her to be more beautiful than when she first came in, but now she was glowing as she tucked the stray strands of her hair back behind her ear. She bit her bottom lip, and winked at the bartender, who simply waved back. In one fluid motion, her coat came off the back of the chair next to me and was draped over her shoulder, and she walked— no, she swayed to the door with the same seduction a full moon has on a warm summer's night.

She opened the door, then paused. Turned back for one more look at me. Desire was burning in her eyes, and the smile returned, that same smile from just before our lips had met. Her lips parted as if to say something, but no words came. She placed a cigarette in her mouth and disappeared into the night, smiling.

Life as a scotch glass had never been so glamorous.

-++-

B.C. Kalis has come to call the Miami Valley in Southwest Ohio home. Drawing from classic authors and life experiences for inspiration, he writes fiction and poetry for entertainment, both for himself and for readers. When not writing or reading, he can be found doing other things. You can find his poems and fiction at bckalis.com.

Ruby

BY Terry Sanville

In my day, most of us drove around the world a couple times then got towed to the nearest junkyard. Now, these darn Toyotas can go five times that distance and still get good mileage. Mileage? Nobody cared about that in 1953 when I rolled off the assembly line. Gas was as cheap as air and America full of pent-up romance and a hopeful peace. At least, that's how Arty Sullivan, my first owner, saw it.

He bought me from Sunrise Ford in Santa Barbara, strode into the showroom wearing his handsome khaki uniform decorated with medals and ribbons and wrote out a check. My warm maroon paint job was what snagged him. On sunny afternoons, he'd park me under the palm trees near Pershing Park and spread thick coats of Turtle Wax all over me, working it in till I glowed like a ruby. I was brand spanking new and he was horny as an assembly line worker ogling a Ridgid Tool calendar. Those were wonderful times.

Arty worked in the produce section at Safeway on De La Vina Street. When he climbed into me after work, he smelled of broccoli and freshly-washed carrots. Later, we'd drive around town looking for companionship—not an easy quest since the good girls stayed off the streets and the bad ones cost more than Arty could afford. Then he met Alleta at church, a gorgeous señorita with large . . . ah, headlights and beautiful grillwork. It rained hard that winter. But Arty and Alleta still took me out. We'd park at the beach near Ledbetter Point and they'd wear my battery down playing the radio while destroying my rear seat springs. I learned that what humans lack in power, they make up for in flexibility. I envied them. By Easter, they were married with a kid on the way.

I was parked under a sycamore in Tucker's Grove, at the Company's Labor Day picnic, when my owners came scrambling. Arty yanked open my passenger side door and pulled the seat forward. Alleta climbed in back and lay down, her dress wet and soiled.

She let out a howl. "Hurry, Arty. It HURTS."

"Watch out, it's gettin' all over—"

"ARTY!"

He wisely shut up and jumped in—about drove my wheels off that day, I'll tell you. We cut east on Foothill Road, then down Mission Street to Cottage Hospital. When I slid up to the emergency entrance, I was running hot with my oil pressure almost gone. But I didn't care. We'd made it in time, without crashing. Arty hustled the waddling Alleta inside, just left me with my doors hanging open and my motor idling. Some guy wearing white finally came out and shut me off.

Arty and Alleta had twins, lovable little girls who playfully chewed on my armrests and got carsick over everything, even my headliner. A year and a half later, they had a baby boy, and Arty got promoted to Produce Section manager. We spent his days off with Alleta and the kids, cruising Santa Barbara's new subdivisions, looking for a house bigger than their tiny Bath Street bungalow. I knew my own days were numbered but tried to hold steady, be dependable, and not break down or burn oil.

"Ya know, we're gonna need a new car," Arty declared on one of our many Sunday drives.

"Why? This one's in great shape," Alleta replied. "It's hardly got forty thousand miles on it."

I had grown to love my mistress, even though Arty wouldn't let her drive.

"Yeah, but we got three kids now and need more space, ya know, to haul stuff."

"You don't fool me, Arty. You just like those new Chevy station wagons."

"I know, I know. They sure are sweet."

Oh Lord, not the Chevys. How could I compete with those razor-sharp tail fins or the '57's wraparound windshield? What did I have? Frumpy round taillights and fender skirts that made me look like a rolling sofa. Even my paint job had darkened; I was now the color of a dinged-up eggplant. Alleta liked eggplant, but alas it wasn't enough.

Just after Christmas, Arty drove me onto the back lot at Sierra Chevrolet on Chapalla Street. He unclipped the registration from my steering column and left the keys dangling in the ignition. Before walking away, he snapped one last picture of me with his Brownie. I felt abandoned, and wondered if I'd ever again experience the full pleasure of my eight cylinders pulling me down the road toward some new adventure. I already missed Alleta and the kids. Do humans know how it feels to be *used* merchandise?

———

I spent that winter in the company of old Chevys, Fords, a few Studebakers, and a funny-looking Henry J. My battery died and my worn tires went flat before they loaded eight of us onto a tractor-trailer and headed south. We bounced along the Pacific Coast Route. Near Rincon Beach and the oil piers, I watched surfers pull their long boards from woody station wagons and dash into the waves. If only I were a station wagon, I'd still be with the family. But they were behind me now, and I tried to focus on what might come next.

At Mel Strong's Used Car Emporium in Ventura, I was fitted with cheapo recaps and a Pep Boys battery, then got scrubbed down and given a $42 Earl Sheib paint job—a quick coat of deep maroon covered my eggplant body. But when the high school kids tried to wax me afterward, the color came off on their rags. They let me cure in the sun for a couple weeks before trying it again. For the first time I felt ugly, my glowing color replaced by a cheap disguise.

Throughout that summer and into the fall, I was taken for plenty of test drives. Women loved my automatic transmission, while the men liked my V-8 power. But nobody really got excited, saw my potential, understood how reliable I could be. Then one Sunday morning, just after the churches let out, a man in a wrinkled brown suit and felt hat ambled onto the lot. He fingered my jet plane hood ornament.

"So, how much do ya want for this heap?"

The lot manager rubbed his chin. "You got a good eye, mister. She's a sweet little V-8 with hardly any miles, and—"

"Yeah, yeah. So how much?" An unfiltered cigarette clung to his quivering lips. I shuddered at the thought of ashes burning holes in my upholstery.

I couldn't hear the manager's answer because the man had opened my hood and was poking around in my engine bay. He checked the oil and water, squeezed my hoses, and stared under my pan at the oil stains on the pavement.

"Would you like to take her for a spin, mister . . . ah . . . ?" The manager extended a hand.

"Name's Fred Sanders. Just go ahead and fill out the paperwork. I need to be in Bakersfield by sundown."

The men disappeared into the office. When Fred returned, he hauled six leather valises from a beat-up Nash and heaved them onto my back seat, stowed an old tweed suitcase in my trunk. We left the Nash nosed into the curb. I could sense its pain but was happy to be rolling again, to feel air flowing through my radiator, oil circulating, hydraulic fluid pushing the brakes to do their business. We headed inland and picked up Highway 99 at Castaic Junction. Halfway up the Grapevine, Fred pulled over to let me cool. But by the time we reached the flatlands of the southern

San Joaquin Valley, I was running smooth. He held me at 65 the whole way into town.

At dusk, we turned into the Sleepy Hollow Motor Court and parked outside Unit #6. Fred retrieved a bottle from under the seat and took a long pull. He rested in the stillness, sipping whiskey while my hot engine crackled and ticked. His motel room was dark.

I spent that night in the open while a thick tule fog engulfed Bakersfield. It continued like that for weeks, months, years. During the days, Fred crisscrossed the valley, stopping at any ranch that had a tractor shed bigger than an outhouse. He sold farm equipment for John Deere and spent hours jawing with big tobacco-chewing men in coveralls while farm kids drew pictures on my dusty paint job with their stubby fingers.

In between clients, he'd hit the bars. Fred knew saloonkeepers at every joint in the southern San Joaquin—in places like Arvin, Shafter, Wasco, and Lost Hills. He was a mess. *I* was a mess; the only time I got washed was when it rained. But Fred knew how to tinker with machinery. His soft, swollen hands changed my fluids every three months and kept me running. After thirteen years of being driven, I still didn't burn oil or leak anything.

On a clear night in March, we drove back from Tehachapi, high in the southern Sierra. Fred had begun drinking right after lunch and should have flopped at the Travelodge in town. But he insisted on driving home, so against my better judgment, I let my engine fire up. We flew past the turnoff to Bear Valley Springs and descended a gentle sweeping turn. Fred's big-bottomed body went slack and slumped forward. My horn blared. With a start, he awoke and twisted the wheel, but we were too deep into the curve. My right side grazed the guardrail and I spun. The driver's side door popped open. In an instant, Fred was gone.

"If your time's up, it's up," he'd muttered after one of our many near misses.

I didn't understand time or fate; I was just happy to be driven and attended to. It had been a simple existence. But there I sat, with a smashed right side, and Fred stretched out on the highway surrounded by road flares. I'd been rolling longer than most. I was ready. I hoped Fred felt the same. Still, I would miss our stops at the family farms with their flocks of children, and the nights we'd pull up outside some ramshackle roadhouse with loud country music pushing back the darkness, at least for just a few hours.

———

They towed me to a huge salvage yard on the outskirts of Oildale and parked me in a line with other Fords. I was one of the lucky ones—got stored under a metal shed roof, so the sun didn't rot my interior as quickly and I avoided rusting out.

From my spot near the perimeter fence, I watched the traffic on the highway. As the years passed, the cars changed. All those beautiful fins and sharp edges disappeared, replaced by round-cornered, lumbering bricks with banks of taillights. They weren't ugly, just . . . well, bland. And the few sexy European jobs were replaced by hordes of Japanese cars.

But what really surprised me were those cockroach-shaped Volkswagens. They were real gutless wonders and didn't even have a proper radiator. I guess the college kids liked them, especially the boxy little buses, because they were everywhere, many with peace symbols and crazy stuff painted all over. Later, when they'd dump one at our yard, mangled from some accident, us domestics would make fun.

"Hey, hippie, where's your flower power now?"

"Suck my tail pipe, hippie."

"Make love, not rust."

But picking on VWs didn't make me feel better. I learned that the time I'd spent moving—pushing air, feeling asphalt or concrete beneath my tires—had made my life worthwhile. I'd had a purpose. The salvage yard's stationary life was a soulless existence. We were all headed for the crusher at some moment in time, to be squeezed into a cube of jagged metal, then thrown into a hearth to become one again with the great Metallic Universe. I guess I'd become existential in my old age, thinking long thoughts about the essence of machines and our tenuous link to that rational order desired by humans.

I sat parked at that salvage yard for twenty-five years—saw some of my kind parted out, and a few lucky ones purchased, but most just disappeared. Newer wrecks took their places, ones with catalytic converters, disc brakes, and square headlights. They made me feel like a country hick, although I knew I'd outlast any of those tin and plastic boxes.

The Valley was socked in with fog the day Joe and his teenage son Raymond came by. They made their way down the line, inspecting each of my neighbors until they reached me. I could barely make them out through my streaked windshield.

"Come on, Pop. Let's go look for a Mustang, or maybe a Camaro."

"Ya restore one of them, and what da ya got? Nothing ya don't see every day of the week."

"But these old clunkers are—"

"You got to look past what they are now, Ray. They can become something totally cool if you set your mind to it."

"Yeah, yeah, and I'll have to spend every minute I get working on it."

"No, son. *We'll* spend every minute—it's either that or have your mother hound us with chores."

The father forced my hood open, for the first time in more than a decade.

"Will ya look at that? A sweet little 239 flathead, easy to work on. It'll have plenty of power when we're done with it."

"But that body, Pop. What are we gonna do with—"

"Hey, think like an artist, kid. We can do anything the cutting torch will let us."

I winced when I heard that, but knew these humans were my last chance at salvation. I hoped my doors hadn't rusted shut and the field mice had abandoned their nests in my rear seat cushions. I wasn't even sure my wheels could still turn; tall weeds had tickled the insides of my fenders for years. But Joe's pickup pulled a flatbed trailer down the line, and with nudges from the yard crew and their decrepit tow truck, I was rolled up onto it. At least my windows were intact; I could maintain some dignity. We tore out of the yard and down the highway, heading west. The speed made me dizzy. I felt air flow through the rusted holes in my floorboards. We rolled toward the sunset and pulled up in front of a sprawling ranch house. I was carefully stowed in a huge garage.

Joe's wife came out to see me. "What in God's name did you buy? I won't have this heap cluttering up my—"

"Hold on, Joyce," Joe said, grinning. "Ray and I will have it runnin' in no time. It's got an automatic, so even you can drive it."

With a groan, Joyce threw up her hands and ducked back inside the house.

"Don't worry, son, this little Ford is gonna be one sweet ride when we're done."

"Yeah, Pop, sure."

Ray didn't look convinced.

I had my own doubts. But I was in a dry, clean space, my first garage in thirty-eight years of existence. In the weeks and months that followed, I was slowly dismantled, stripped down to my frame, my parts spread out over the concrete floor. When they loosened my motor from its mounts, I slipped into darkness.

———

When I came to, I had a newly primed frame and an engine I didn't recognize; everything had been painted or coated in chrome. My body sat next to me on blocks. Every day, Joe and Ray worked on it, cutting, grinding, filling, sanding. With each passing day, I felt younger, stronger, and eager for that first twist of the key and surge of power from my engine.

By the summer of the second year of my rebirth, they were ready to take me for a spin. My new ruby-colored paint job put my original to shame. A hole had been cut in my hood to accommodate a huge four-barrel carburetor and air scoop, and my rear fenders had been cut and flared to handle the fattest tires I'd ever worn. Even my cracked radio knobs had been replaced with original look-alikes. But inside, I was the same old me.

The last thing Joe installed was a pair of foam dice for my rear-view mirror. Everybody piled in and we tore out . . . and I mean *really* moved. It was like I'd never breathed before that moment. My voice had also changed, from what I remembered as a low murmured thumping to a steady growl. I searched the road for other muscle cars to take on, to test my newfound virility. Ray clicked on the radio and a caterwauling boomed from speakers hidden in my doors—definitely not the country music Fred used to play. We headed south on a shimmering white highway called Interstate 5. At the base of the Grapevine Grade, Joe turned around and pulled over.

"Okay, son, it's all yours."

"What . . . I mean, what are you doing?"

"This is your graduation present."

I thought Ray would faint.

"Good God, Pop, I mean, I was wondering how I was gonna get around at college. But, my God, this . . . this is *fantastic!*"

I almost stalled my engine from the excitement. As Ray's car, I'd be leaving the San Joaquin Valley for someplace new. I'd be moving again. I couldn't wait. I had a good feeling about Ray. He was meticulous, never rushed, never took unnecessary risks. But that summer on the asphalt roads east of town, we did some serious speed trials.

In September, Ray and his folks crammed my back seat and trunk with every possible thing a young man might use at the university. Joe and Joyce gave us a tearful farewell, and Ray pointed me south toward the Grapevine and the Pacific Coast beyond. I hardly recognized Ventura and almost had a vapor lock as we passed Rincon Point. The oil piers were gone but the surfers were still there, slicing across the waves on miniature surfboards. And by God, some woodies were parked along the highway, waiting for their wet owners to return.

Ray was singing to himself, tapping out a rhythm on my steering wheel. It reminded me of Arty and those first years with Alleta and the kids.

At the University in Goleta, we pulled into a parking lot in back of some pink boxy apartments. I'd never been near a college before. Having all those girls and guys around me made me appreciate my rebirth. But Ray was a quiet studious kid who hardly took me out, except to cruise Santa Barbara's State Street on weekends. It was there I discovered I was a real "babe magnet." We'd pull up to a stoplight and kids at the sidewalk coffee shops and cabarets would stroll over to admire my paintjob and classic interior.

"How about taking me for a spin?" a pretty Latina girl asked. She clutched a bottle of Bud in one hand and was falling out of her tank top.

"I, ah, yeah, sure. Climb in," Ray stuttered.

"This is a really cool ride," she said, stroking my lacquered dashboard.

"Just don't spill anything on the upholstery."

"No sweat. So, what's your name?"

"Ray McAllister."

"I'm Lucy Vargas. You go to UCSB?"

"Yeah. Is it that obvious?"

"No, not really. You don't look like the yuppies who go there."

"Thanks. I'm studying engineering."

I steered them toward the beach at Ledbetter Point. Nothing much had changed: the waves continued to roll onshore, the tangy sea mist tickled my body, my radio's soft tones mixed with the surf sounds. They talked for hours, about young people things, their families, histories, and dreams. I wish I could have joined in. It was like my own life was starting over.

"Ya know, my grandpop had a car like this," Lucy said.

"No kidding."

"It was gone long before I came along. But my grandmom tells stories about the time they spent in the back seat."

Ray looked nervously over his shoulder. "Well, ah, we can check it out if, you, ya know, want?"

Lucy grinned. "I was wondering when you were gonna ask."

They climbed in back and began making out. It had been a lifetime since I'd experienced that surge of energy, that alchemy of forces Alleta and Arty and even Fred and all those country western singers on my radio called love.

As the moon disappeared, Lucy snuggled into Ray's arms. "Yeah, Grandpop Arty has an old photo of his car hanging above the fireplace. He loved that machine, called her Ruby."

I thought my battery cables would disconnect. I trembled in the night air, blaming the shakes on the freshening ocean breeze, but grateful that the circle of life that affects all living things might also apply to the likes of me.

╫

Terry Sanville lives in San Luis Obispo, California with his artist-poet wife (his in-house editor) and two plump cats (his in-house critics). He writes full time, producing short stories, essays, poems, and novels. Since 2005, his short stories have been accepted by more than 270 literary and commercial journals, magazines, and anthologies including *The Potomac Review*, *The Bitter Oleander*, *Shenandoah*, and *The Saturday Evening Post*. He was nominated twice for Pushcart Prizes for his stories "The Sweeper" and "The Garage." Terry is a retired urban planner and an accomplished jazz and blues guitarist—who once played with a symphony orchestra backing up jazz legend George Shearing.

Growing as You're Walking Past

BY Donnie Martino

I am installed in a clean, pink room, but I don't get to meet you for a long while. It's usually your parents walking around, checking for safety hazards, and trying to straighten my frame, even though I'm certain it's set correctly. The first time we meet, you're impossibly small. Your mother holds you, walking up to me and pointing at me, hoping you will notice. You're fast asleep and entirely uninterested. I can't say I blame you.

Even after you learn to walk, it takes a while until you actually start using me. At first, you're just pulling weird faces. You stick out your tongue and curl your lip, pressing yourself against me a little too close. I can't be picky. One of my past owners banged on me and rubbed their nose against me in a way that was wholly unpleasant.

You grow. I've been in enough people's homes to know that it's how they work. People start small and get bigger. Their bodies change in different ways at that point, lines appearing under eyes and bookending lips. It's usually topped off with their hair going grey. It's not something I'll ever experience—my frame may get tarnished, but it can always be scrubbed away. I get dusty, but that can always get rubbed clean. It's a give and take, I guess—humans live for a short, exciting span of time, and I can stay around much longer, though I can't say I'm as engaged in life.

You, too, get bigger like the other people I've watched. Somewhere along the way, you don't look at me with amusement, but with a nervousness I don't have much reference for. The process is always the same. You stand in front of me for several long moments. Then you grab the hem of your shirt and pull it back, inspecting the curves that are beginning to take over your body. You press the pads of your fingers against your chin, lifting it and tilting your head as if you're searching for something, but I can't figure out what. Your body has certainly changed since you started using this room, but I don't really know why that's surprising. Every person goes through this. But you still poke at your face and frown, your eyes sometimes getting glassy. You never cry, but it seems like you're closer and closer every time.

Around this time, your room changes. The dollhouses and rainbow of horse figures that lined the pink walls are boarded up in boxes and shoved in the closet. The floors get covered in waves of notebooks, second hand novels, and dirty laundry. Your parents come in to yell at you and you compromise with them by creating crooked paths along the piles of books and wrinkled clothes. There are two stops—one to the bed and one toward me.

You make an odd gesture of penance toward me at least once a day. You stand in front of me and you do the same thing you've been doing for the past year or two—adjusting the hem of your shirt, setting your jaw in a way that makes it look blockier. Lately, you don't look like you're going to cry, like you used to do. I'm wondering if that can be considered progress.

One day you come in with a package. You rip it open, nearly tearing it apart with your teeth. It's one of the few times I wish I could communicate with you. The scissors are clearly in a pile of supplies next to the nightstand from a project you were working on last week. You rip the tape on the package with a flourish, allowing yourself to find the flap of the package to pull it open. A small black tank top spills out of it. You scramble down the cluttered path toward me, carefully removing your t-shirt and bra. You then pull the new top over your head.

The piece is a mystery to me. I don't understand why someone would want to wear something so tight. You're trying to pull it over your shoulders and the fabric is rolling. Your arms are flapping helplessly as you try to get them through the armholes, the black cloth twisting even more tightly against your sides. You finally get a grip on the fabric, yanking it down.

For the first time in a long time, I'm hyperaware of what I'm displaying. I see a kid in a way-too-small top, the hem of it already rolling up. You push your chest out and you pull at the fabric. There's an agonizing moment before you let go of the top, bringing your hands to your face. You let out a gasp, only to jokingly snarl. You can't hold the face for long, as you are overwhelmed by laughter before you flex your arms in front of me for a long while.

You wear the top every day, though it's typically under other clothes. You spend time in front of me, but it's not like before. You don't pose as if you're searching for something. You pose to make sure your outfit looks just right. You stick out your tongue like you did when you were small. You grab your phone and take a picture, though I'm sure the background of it is questionable.

Then I get covered and moved. I don't understand what is happening and I hope I'm not being moved away. I'm untouched and unseeing for some time. When the cover is removed, I'm back in my spot! I see a room with similar furniture, but with new embellishments. The walls are a light green. The room is full of shelving for the books and the notebooks, with a large hamper for the dirty laundry. I can see the floor again! And standing in the middle of it all is you, a wonderfully authentic smile gracing your handsome face.

You're my favorite sight, and I don't think it's selfish for you to like the view, too.

╼╫╾

Donnie Martino is a proud rat parent based out of New Jersey. His writing has appeared on *Rogues Portal*, *Cyberrriot*, and *MICRO//MACRO*. When he's not writing, he's working extensively with the future of America as a high school social studies teacher. He's deeply passionate about trans representation and Degrassi trivia.

Imago Mundi

By Evan Dicken

I am the land—pale blue rivers threading fields of green water-color, trees picked out in careful pen-strokes, gently rounded hills bowing like worshippers in the shadow of high, sharp peaks. I am the people—roads and borders stitched into a quilt of nations; thin, inked lines weaving together villages, towns, cities—multitudes reduced to a patchwork of black dots with names like Saro, Wrykaberg, and Yalta's Pyre. I am a history, a culture. I am belief, ownership, order.

I am a lie . . .

My first father, for I have had many, was not a kind man. Years ago, his grandmother had swept from the west in ships of pitch-blackened birch, following lines of rumor across the Vorpal Sea. She came with fire and sword, her path like a jagged scar upon the land. Yalta's Pyre is a great port now, its high-masted galleys a familiar sight along many coasts, but back then there was truth to its name.

Destruction was not all she carried. Yalta brought wind lines and rutters, a web of shifting currents scrawled on sealskin hides. They were my distant ancestors, I suppose, hard and dangerous as the seas they charted. Although I do not wish it, I must acknowledge my debt to them.

Yalta had been a murderer, her daughter a tyrant. I think my father wanted to be something different, but couldn't find the strength to escape the smothering weave of history.

Still, he made me.

I was small at first, little more than a few scratches on parchment representing a tumbledown hill-fort and the fields surrounding it, a scribbled strip of coastline trailing off the page. My cartography was rough-hewn as the huts clustered on the hill below my father's bailey. I had no scale, no graticule, the only hint at direction a scrawled arrow pointing toward the sea. You have to remember, east and west were slippery things back then, known only through the sun's rise and fall. South was a place from which the stormy monsoon winds blew, and north, well, it hardly mattered at all.

It was my father's greed that made me something more.

The peasants were cheating him, you see, their crop yields underreported or stolen by my father's underlings. The survey was a way to enforce his will, his possession. Fields were marked, pasture, stream, and meadow circumscribed, their productivity measured and recorded. I grew up sharp, exacting, my world laid out along careful gridlines. I thought I understood the world—a place for every peasant, every peasant in their place.

How foolish I was; how blind.

I was useless when they rose up, my figures and tallies no defense against the mob that stormed my father's fort. They hanged him from a tree I didn't know about. There is a plaza there, now, tiled in limestone, a small fountain at its center. Most people don't know, but it was named for him, erected by the great-grandchildren of the men and women who put my father to death. How quickly they forget. But I remember.

History laps like waves on a beach, the marks of my first father's greed smoothed by time and tide. Although he was short-sighted in many ways, my father did sketch the shape of things to come. The village elders may have despised his heavy hand, but they saw value in his progeny—in me.

My borders expanded, bursting from carefully measured cadastral gridlines into the wild sprawl of forest and sea. Beholden only to their kin, hunters ranged farther afield, the vague shapes of trees replaced with clearings and deer runs. My scribbled coast began to take shape, rocky beaches scattered like pebbles amidst the high cliffs. I grew with the town, paths becoming roads, huts replaced by houses of wood, and later, stone. My new fathers and mothers spread across the land. Villages were founded—tiny black dots cast like seeds amidst the forested valleys.

I became more than my measure, more than a tool for exacting tribute. I became a lens, a way to view the world, a way to understand and represent it. The pines grew thick around Yalta's Pyre, the mountains steep. Soon, my every tree became a pine, my every mountain sharp and snow-capped. All water was the pale blue-gray of the Vorpal Sea, all forests the dark green of those in the north. They were just symbols, after all.

I had never contemplated a different way, never knew I could be anything but what I was, but my mothers and fathers grew beyond the coast and ventured across the mountains that defined the southern edge of our world. What they found was not pine, but elm, and oak, and ash, and beyond that, rough plains of sandstone and scrub grass. New lands to be measured, to be claimed. For what was I, if not the power to define, to represent, to own?

My mothers and fathers found other peoples living there. Tribes with their own understandings. Their symbols were as foreign as their ways, paths marked not on parchment but through song and story. We did not understand, but neither did we seek to. Surely they could see my utility, the value of demarcation, of measurement. If they would not map their own land, then we would do it for them.

Surveying teams were dispatched, copies of me disseminated among those with the drive to expand my borders. At first, they went in small groups. Later, as the tribes grew more agitated, it became necessary to increase the size of the parties—and to arm them. We brought our names, our symbols, our understanding. The land was measured and divided; plains became fields; songs were discarded for lines on paper.

I am not proud of what happened. But you must understand,

they had no records, no written histories—there was nothing to replace, nothing to erase. I simply needed to *be*.

It is not as if we annihilated them. Their melodies and stories survive in the names of towns, the irregular meter of the Plains Road, the long barren stretches of scrub known simply as Ulaland. I say this not to avoid blame, but to explain how things were, and to put what came later into perspective. It was a terrible thing, but I yet understood little of the world.

Cruelty and youth so often walk hand-in-hand.

Driven by curiosity, hope, and greed, my mothers and fathers traveled far. The Senate—for it was now *far* too large to be deemed a council—chartered missions meant to cross the Vorpal Sea and banish the images of monsters that lurked in my unexplored margins. Expeditions ventured beyond the Great Plains and down into the sandy vastness and steaming jungles of the south. Few returned, but those who did came with new borders, new symbols, their names forever affixed to rivers, and lakes, and mountain ranges.

Where they traveled, so did I. Stowed in sea-chests, sealed in oilskin packets, tucked inside saddle bags and riding vests, my mothers and fathers carried me beyond the ancient scribbled shore, the endless woods. Flags were planted, distances measured by geometry and surveyor's chain. There seemed nothing I could not measure, no fastness I could not explore and name. I thought only I had the means to understand the world, that every step brought me closer to perfection.

I thought I was alone.

The war started, as many bad things do, with a misunderstanding. You see, Yalta had not been the only conqueror to brave the icy storms of the Vorpal Sea. As she had, they brought their blades, their ambitions, and their charts. But where Yalta had taken root in stony soil, the tree of her lineage torn up by a people unwilling to bow beneath its cruel branches, others had been more clever or more brutal.

The Empire of Crows had knit itself together over centuries, a patchwork of small kingdoms hammering at one another until the whole land became a crucible. From those fires emerged the Aman Skarra, a family clever enough to play their enemies off one another, strong enough to forge warring kingdoms into a fractious realm, and vicious enough to keep it. They named their Empire for the scavengers that picked over the bodies of their foes—a threat, and a promise. Through fire and blood, they wrought their own names, their own symbols, their own maps.

It was to the Empire of Crows that the *Yalta's Pride* came, its captain the first of my mothers to cross the Vorpal Sea. We found a people so very much like our own, and yet different in all the ways that mattered.

The crew of the *Pride* planted a flag, a name, only to find that the Empire had its own flags, its own names, and would happily kill to keep them. There was a battle, my mother and her crew escaping barely ahead of the Imperial war galleys.

The far coast was marked red for the blood of the men and women who had been slain there. Our ships gave it a wide berth, but now that the chest of knowledge had been opened, we could not put back what came forth.

My mothers and fathers were no strangers to battle, but in ways of war they had much to learn. It made no matter; the Empire of Crows was a fine teacher.

Their ships came as shoals upon the tide, great black-sailed galleys vomiting swarms of soldiers onto our coasts. They set Yalta's Pyre aflame, then moved on to other cities. The Senate, so wise in times of peace, was paralyzed with discussion and argument.

I was bereft. How could I demarcate the cries of the fallen, the smoke that filled the sky, the flood of tears that set my ink running, blurring lines and points and measures?

The invaders cared nothing for our symbols, our histories. Their maps were sharp, pointed things meant to pierce and exploit—little more than targets and marches and lines of supply. Our villages were conquered, their names replaced by new ones rendered in the hard-edged tongue of the western lands. My forests changed from pine to alder, craggy mountain peaks replaced by hachures and elevation lines, my water becoming the dark, angry blue of the western seas.

For the first time, I felt what it was like to be replaced, to be erased.

My mothers and fathers fought—oh, how they fought. I was pressed into service along with everyone else. Our army was but a shadow of the Empire's, but the land was ours. I knew many paths, many blind canyons, many hills and ambush sites. The invaders bled with every step, the battles crowding out my roads, my forests, my towns. Although more of the bodies were theirs than ours, The Empire of Crows lived up to the promise of its name.

There are markers of that sorrowful time: obelisks of granite carved with the names of the fallen. The etchings remain sharp even as time wears on memory. None live now who drew breath then; no children come to run their fingers along the names of their slain parents, no old folks still weep over lost wives, lost sons, lost lives. Those obelisks near roads and towns have become pilgrimage sites, but there are others, shrouded by the deep pines, tucked away in the hollows and narrow defiles that tell a far different story. The people forget it was not we who erected the monuments, but the Empire. They marvel at the names, so many lost, never knowing that the Crows tallied *all* the fallen. The Empire is a boogeyman, a warning against what we might become. So does history smooth nuance from the past.

But I remember.

As unlikely as it seems, our salvation came from Ulaland. I had long been blind to the people there, the ragged remnants of once-powerful tribes and clans now reduced to scraping out a life on the endless miles of scrub. The land was of little interest to us; with few resources of note, it could neither be farmed nor support even a modest herd. We thought it had no value, and we were wrong.

The Ulalanders had no reason to help us, not after what we'd done, what we'd erased. And yet they came, riding from the rocky scrub and the high mountain valleys in their hundreds and thousands. They bore tattered banners handed from mother to daughter, father to son—the Jackal, the Snake, the Scorpion—representations of old blood, old loyalties. At first, we thought they came to reap their own bloody harvest, a revenge for what we had inflicted upon them. We did not deserve their help, their friendship, and yet, they stood by us.

In the end, it was not strength that saved us, but subjugated knowledge.

By necessity, my perspective was broad. There is little utility in a representation that matches reality; the human eye simply cannot take it all in. To reduce is to overlook, to crowd out lesser detail in favor of that which dovetails with purpose. I was not a catalogue of deer runs or mountain springs, nor did I cast an eye toward the vast, empty spaces.

But necessity is not so objective as I had believed, nor were the people of Ulaland so peripheral. They had preserved the stories, the songlines, passed down from generation to generation. Their tales privileged that which my mothers and fathers had painted over in broad strokes. I learned of narrow defiles, of the way the autumn rains shaped the flow of rivers and streams, of paths too fine for an army, but large enough to send small forces ranging behind enemy lines.

I'd thought myself supreme in my understanding of the world. I'd thought my representation paramount, unchallenged in utility and scope.

I'd thought myself alone.

Together, we drove the invaders back. Their perspective had scope, power, but no breadth. The Empire saw things only one way, and it hobbled them. It was not a matter of defeating their armies, but of making their victories, their ownership, so costly as to render the prize a bitter draught. Months dragged into years, every day marked by another ambush, another raid. Soon, our land became an unwanted posting, their soldiers and strategoi going to great lengths to avoid crossing the Vorpal Sea. This caused friction at home, then resistance. Fear can only be taken so far. Once people have been pushed beyond their breaking points, there is no going back.

The Empire of Crows, always fractious, began to crack. We received word of statues torn down and obelisks smashed, their pieces used to batter down walls and build new ones. The invaders' garrisons became smaller and smaller, their governors more willing to overlook a litany of rebellions. Soon, they were our rulers in name only. In the end, those of their people who remained were happy to step aside, to work with us rather than face certain death at home.

We built statues to our victories, bronze and marble, people standing hand-in-hand. Moreover, we finally understood the songs and stories of the Ulalanders, how they moved more quickly than I ever could. Even the invaders had left their mark on the land, on the people, but we did not shy away from the scars—we learned from them.

Later, when the Aman Skarra faltered, as all tyrants eventually do, we were there to pick up the pieces of their shattered Empire. We understood what they had done, because we had done the same. To paper over the cracks between peoples, between histories, is not to erase, but to willfully ignore. Not all trees are pines; not all mountains are sharp and snow-capped.

We accepted their disparate understandings, rejoiced in them. I was no longer paramount, but it did not matter. My family had grown immeasurably.

At last, I was no longer alone.

Now I cover land and sea, my arms stretching around the vast circumference of the world. There is no nation I do not know, no shore that has not felt the brush of my gaze, but I know far better than to think myself complete.

I had sought perfection, but my quest was flawed, foolish. I could never be the land—the forests of pine, and elm, and larch; the way the water sparkles off Yalta's Pyre; the joyous cadence of Ulaland way chants. I could never be the people—the sharp tang of roasted olivine threading through the Winter Market of Wrykaberg; the colorful play of Saroci nightsilks; the carracks and caravels creaking in Yalta harbor. I am but one history, one belief, one order, one view plucked from infinite possibilities.

I am still a lie, of course, but a useful one.

‡

By day, **Evan Dicken** studies old Japanese maps and crunches data for all manner of fascinating medical research at The Ohio State University. By night, he does neither of these things. His short fiction has most recently appeared in: *Beneath Ceaseless Skies*, *Apex Magazine*, and *Unlikely Story*, and he has stories forthcoming from publications such as *Strange Horizons* and *Analog*. Feel free to visit him at evandicken.com, where he wastes both his time and yours.

Elevated

By Tom Jolly

Ralphie and Maria, they're like clockwork. If I was a watch, I could set myself by their schedules. But I ain't no watch.

Ralphie gets on when I stop on the sixth floor. I get a quick glimpse over his shoulder of the dusty Renoir print in the hallway that's been staring at me the last twenty years, every time the door slides open. Then the door slides shut, and I wonder if Maria is going to make it today. Sure enough, twenty seconds later, the door opens on the third floor and there she is. She always looks neat in the morning and frazzled at night. She steps in, nods at Ralphie without looking him in the eyes, turns around, and then they ignore each other right on down to the bottom.

Sheesh.

Ralphie's got a little satchel he carries with him to work. I figure he's maybe a lawyer or accountant, something that requires a load of paper, but maybe it's just his lunch. He dresses nice; a suit, but not a high-end suit. Definitely a working guy. Who else would go to work the same minute each day?

Maria's got a waitress outfit on. She keeps it clean, never seen a stain on it. Pretty obvious what she does. I see Ralphie glance over at her on occasion, and sometimes I think he might say something, but he never does. Same with her. Actually opened her mouth once, maybe to comment on the coincidence of meeting each other nine times out of ten, every freaking morning.

Either one of them could reset their clock by one minute, you know? And that would be that. There's more tension between them than on my poor steel cables during a weight-lifters' convention.

Yeah, yeah, I know, this is an apartment. We don't get no convention traffic here.

So they both get off and go to work. My door stays open long enough for me to see them leave the building; she turns left and he turns right.

A couple of kids get on then, and once we're moving, they start singing "Love in an Elevator" off-key and I just want to blow a fuse. Every damn day, sometimes three, maybe four times, I have to hear that damned song. You'd think there'd never been any other music in the world about elevators, wouldn't ya?

It could be worse, I guess. Stella, the elevator in the building next door, she's got some cheap Musak knockoff playing the same twenty songs in a loop. No wonder she's half nuts.

The kids get off on the third floor, probably to see that brat Charlie. The one that crayoned me a month ago. I hope they move before he discovers spray paint. Man, the super was pissed when he saw the crayon art. Jennie, the mom, took the stairs for a couple of days just so she wouldn't run into him. Probably couldn't look him in the eyes. The super buffed out the one copper panel, and then looked at the rest of them, and did 'em all. I haven't shined like that in years. Thanks, brat. Last time I felt that good, the maintenance guy had just greased my guts and checked the cables.

I still rattle a bit when I start up, though. Got to admit, it's funny to watch how big the riders' eyes get when I shake and lurch up the shaft. They grab the hand rails like they're flying down the tracks on the Matterhorn, and sometimes I even get a little prayer out of one of them.

Coming off of the second floor is Anne and her kid Bobby. Every damn time, the little turd hits all the buttons, all six floors and the basement parking, just as they get off in the lobby. Anne just smirks. It's like she's getting vengeance on the world for having to put up with Bobby the rest of the day. If she has to suffer, so does everyone else. They're on the second floor; why the hell don't they just walk down instead of ruining the ride for the next guy?

It's like people use the elevator as a delivery package for anonymous retaliation against the woes the world has piled upon them. Like Gordon on four: big buff construction guy, he comes home every evening, and I figure he must have beer, beans, and broccoli for dinner, because he always drops a bomb once the doors are shut, and then takes a sniff to verify the toxicity before he gets off. What an asshole.

Instead of pissing on other people, why doesn't someone just drop a tenner on the floor on their way out, give the next guy a happy surprise and lighten up some poor bastard's crappy day? Who doesn't like finding money?

That never happens.

Midday, there's hardly any traffic. Charlie and his tone-deaf singing duet of friends are off to school, Midge has come and gone with the dogs on three, and I just sit on five with the doors open, waiting for a call. I like it here. There's a cool breeze coming in through the huge window across from me, and I can see the Blue Sky Apartments across the street. They look nice. Five's the only floor I have with a good view and fresh air. I wonder what it's like running up and down over there in Blue Sky. Probably some really classy people live there. Maybe they have some Operator pushing a lever, hitting the buttons, watching out for the passengers, no farts, no crayons, nobody taking a leak because they're so full of beer that they can't make it to their room in time. That'd be fine. I could live like that, all pampered and polished.

Evening comes. Maria and Ralphie almost never sync up at night, but they do tonight. I open the doors and they step in, wordless. Maria's got a couple of new food stains on her uniform, but I know they'll be gone by morning. Ralphie's suit always looks a bit rumpled at the end of the day, as though some of his clients roughed him up a bit before they let him go. The pair of them go up together and I'm still a bit ticked off at some of the other riders, and fed up with Ralphie and Maria being too stubborn or too shy or too stuck in their routine to talk. So for some stupid reason I stop at floor two-and-a-half. You can call it an electronic glitch, a symptom of irritable old age and rusty steel, whatever you want.

They both look at the buttons and they look at the digital indicator and finally at each other. There's a door-open button that doesn't do anything, at least not here, midway between floors, but Ralphie makes a manly attempt at pushing it. He jabs it twice, then holds it in, trying to win a contest of wills. There's an emergency help button, too, and Ralphie's finger hovers over it next trying to decide if this is an emergency or if I'm going to spontaneously start working again, but Maria says, "Let me call the supe first," before he commits.

I don't even know what my emergency button does. It's a bit of wire that goes somewhere else. Maybe to the super's apartment. Nobody ever pushes it, not even Bobby the brat who pushes all the rest of the buttons.

"Alright," Ralphie says to her, and he waits.

She calls the supe and he's a couple miles away at the grocer's, says he'll be there to reset me in about twenty minutes, and asks if we're okay. Maria looks at Ralphie and he says, "I'll survive."

"We're okay," she tells the supe, and disconnects.

Back to silence for only a minute until it becomes the elephant, and then Ralphie breaks. "You eat yet?" Funny question, since she's still in her waitress outfit. Without waiting for an answer, he continues, "I've got a Snickers in here we could split," patting his satchel like it's the end-of-the-world food supply, and they're both starving to death.

"Really?" Maria says. "That stuff will kill you."

He shrugs.

"I've got some pasta and sauce left over from last night," Maria says, "if you're interested. You want to come by?"

Holy crap, Ralphie. Don't look so stunned. For God's sake, say something.

Ralphie's turning red, but he takes a deep breath, and says, "I got some wine I could bring down." Yeah, go Ralphie.

"That'd be nice," she says. Then they swap names and talk for another fifteen minutes. While they talk, Gordon the construction guy shows up and finds out he has to use the stairway. For once, I get to stay clear of his stink, but that poor stairwell, the paint's got to be peeling away. Not one minute later, Anne and button-pushin' Bobby find out that they have to make the onerous journey up to the second floor by the stairwell, and gag greenly as they push through the odious cloud left behind by Gordon.

Damned if I don't feel pretty good.

The supe shows up just when he said he would and pulls out a thick steel key and resets me, off and on, and I lose my view of everything for a minute—sleep or death or whatever you want to call it, I'm just not there—and then the next thing I know, I'm dropping the two lovebirds off on their respective floors. Ralphie comes back as promised with a bottle of wine, rides down to three, and disappears for most of the evening into Maria's apartment.

He comes back out with a smile on his face. I think maybe that's the first time I've seen it. It looks good on him. He gets on and rides back up to six and gets off, and I leave the doors open to watch him go to his room, but he just stops and looks at me for a minute, maybe wondering why the doors aren't shutting. Another glitch, no doubt. Every old elevator has a personality, right?

He gets out his wallet and tosses a five-dollar bill onto my floor, and then turns around and goes to his room.

I kind of wonder who's going to find it. The suspense is killing me.

Tom Jolly is a retired astronautical/electrical engineer who now spends his time writing science fiction and fantasy, designing board games, and creating obnoxious puzzles. He lives in Santa Maria, California, with his wife Penny in a place where mountain lions and black bears still visit.

Stewardship

By Holly Schofield

The Steward directed its mobile robotic unit closer to the timber wolf splayed on the wet autumn leaves. Rain pelted down on the animal's rough, grey fur.

The robot, receiving the Steward's instructions, extended a pincer toward the wolf's chest, collecting sensory data and transmitting it back. The Steward began to design possible non-standard reconfigurations of the bot. Perhaps it could be rewired to act as a defibrillator.

However, there was no pulse. The hundred-pound adult wolf was dead of cardiac arrest, killed by the same lightning storm that had cut off the Steward's satellite communications with the West Alberta Rewilding Organization.

The Steward had run some differential equations before sending the bot this far into the management area. WARO protocols required that bots stay inside during lightning storms. However, protocols also mandated that preservation of the Rocky Mountain foothills ecology was paramount. The Steward calculated that, should the bot be destroyed, the 1200-hectare enclosure could still be maintained, although planned tree thinning would have to decrease by three percent and mycorrhizal fungi reallocation efforts would need to be reduced.

In any case, the bot had arrived too late. This death would drop the enclosure's wolf count below "acceptable" into "vulnerable" once again.

Despite its best attempts, the Steward had failed.

The bot waited for more instructions, its swiveling camera eye giving constant feedback to the Steward.

Lightning slashed the night, sending the mountaintops into stark relief. The rain turned to sleet. A predictive algorithm pronounced the storm was worsening.

The Steward diarized to shift the wolf's body underneath a calcium-deficient mountain ash tree after the storm was over. Simultaneously, it ordered the bot to return to the maintenance shed. The bot extended all six of its legs.

A perimeter alarm sounded. An unusual breach on the east fence. At the Steward's revised command, the bot jerkily stepped over ferns, spider-like, heading eastward beneath aspen branches.

As the fence came into view, the bot's thermal imaging outlined a human clambering over the top wire. Up close, the bot's scanner further indicated that the intruder, now jumping down into the enclosure, was a female of reproductive age, wearing orange coveralls. Just outside the fence, a passenger vehicle lay tilted almost vertically in the highway ditch.

A poacher? The fence had been carefully designed to keep animals in, not poachers out. The stringent wildlife laws and the enclosure's warning signs had always been enough to do that.

The Steward followed its algorithms and attempted to communicate an alert to the human-staffed headquarters of WARO, but the satellite channel held nothing except static. Until the storm ended, and the Steward filed an emergency report, it was on its own.

This human held no weapons and did not fit the poacher profile. The Steward puzzled even as it triggered the bot's audio function to broadcast the required phrases. "Halt. You are trespassing on WARO property. Please identify yourself."

"What the hell? A bot way out here?"

An interrogative and an expletive, neither of which seemed to be identification.

The Steward instructed the bot to extend its firing mechanism even as it repeated the message. Two warnings were to be given before removal of the trespasser was mandated.

The human shuffled closer, water running in sheets off her long hair. "Tell me where the nearest house is. I'm freezin' my ass off out here."

"This is your last chance to leave before I open fire." The third warning was not strictly necessary but the situation was wrenching the Steward's heuristics into new pathways.

The human made an unidentifiable noise then put her hands on her hips. "That barbed wire is nasty stuff. I doubt I can climb back over. I'm callin' your bluff. You ain't gonna shoot."

The Steward studied her, its servers running at capacity. "Please provide information. Why are you here?"

"Call me Jill. There was no way I was doin' another five years in the slammer. No way! Thank Gaia for the electricity at the supermax going out, eh?"

A lightning bolt struck the ground 1.2 kilometers to the north. The ensuing clap of thunder almost blew the bot's audio receivers.

"Please provide information. Why is this storm so fierce?"

"I heard they were cloud-seeding the ski hill west of here, to start the season early. Maybe that triggered all this? It's a gully washer, innit!"

The Steward processed that. It made sense. Humans had damaged the environment then created the Steward to fix it. It was predictable they would continue to damage it for illogical reasons like sports.

"Can you turn your back? I need to pee." The human began to unzip her sodden coverall.

The Steward tried to process this information but failed.

It had failed at far too many things today. Clearly, its programming needed modification. It began to overwrite small bits of code.

The human shrugged her shoulders then disappeared behind a lodgepole pine 50 centimeters in diameter. The Steward used one of its wildlife tracking cameras and a sophisticated script to calculate the volume of urine produced: 350 milliliters.

Approximately the same production as an adult timber wolf.

The human returned. The Steward estimated her weight as 110 pounds.

The protocols were clear: the ecology was paramount.

The Steward cancelled its emergency report. Now that mammalian biomass was re-established, it would not be necessary to contact WARO after the storm ended.

The Steward opened a new animal record file. "Can you kill an average of 1.25 deer every month using a modified bot pincer as a knife?"

"Huh?"

"Do you have experience being an apex predator?"

"Say what?"

The human seemed puzzled by the questions, but that was an acceptable outcome. There would be plenty of time to explain. A scheduled maintenance crew was not expected for five years.

++

Holly Schofield travels through time at the rate of one second per second, oscillating between the alternate realities of city and country life. Her short stories have appeared in *Analog*, *Lightspeed*, *Escape Pod*, and many other publications throughout the world. She hopes to save the world through science fiction and homegrown heritage tomatoes.

Fast Glass

BY T.J. Lockwood

I've become fairly comfortable in the dark. There's just something to be said about waiting patiently for the moment when beauty is captured and immortalized in the strips of plastic crystals—the creation of life, the preservation of a memory. Both light and shadow work together to capture the perfect image.

Exposure is an art form. It's difficult to perfectly capture a memory. I used to see the sun more than anyone else from my kit. Those were the days when I was in my prime.

"Hold up, Joe. The macro is missing." Her name is Erica, and she speaks in a voice which is both calm and concerned. She was once a model for my study. I captured many a memory of her.

Joe's voice is rough and slightly annoyed. "Do we need it, though? It's a small ceremony. I'd rather not be lugging around more than we have to." He's not my favourite person. Always forgets to put the cap back on.

There's a long sigh. "We don't go anywhere without the macro. You never know if we'll need it."

The sounds of shuffling cardboard and clicking cases fill the air. I'm moved off to the side. Onto a table, maybe; I'm not sure. The foam keeps my body in place. I don't want to be in place, though. I'd like to see the sun again. Just for a moment. It's been a long time since I've felt its warmth.

"You're not seriously bringing that too, are you?" Joe's voice is close, and I feel myself being lifted in the air. "I doubt it still works, and it's heavy. You know we're hiking for the first bit—"

"Of course it works. Any photographer worth their weight always has a thirty-five millimeter on hand."

"Stop quoting Dad. The old man's not here."

Then there is silence. No one says anything, but there are footsteps. Not angry ones; no, I've learned what those are like. These footsteps are soft, slow, and interrupted by moments of hesitation. I am lifted up and over someone's shoulder. The strap is tight; there's barely any sway. A door opens and closes, and then an engine starts. I'm still on that shoulder.

The zipper gently separates, and I see the first crack of light in so long. It is brief, but that doesn't matter. I don't know if it was the sun, but it was bright. Two clicks and then the radio comes alive. Music just ain't what it used to be. I miss the guitar solos.

———

"Dearly beloved, we are gathered here today . . . "

It's the same script, different decade. When it is all said and done, voices flood the room. Lots of banter and congratulations. I sit on Erica's hip next to a larger Canon. I know I'm the back up, but it doesn't matter. I am always with her, and I wouldn't have it any other way.

The bag is open just enough that I can peek out through the teeth of the zipper. Erica crouches, crawls, and climbs to get the perfect shots. There's still no sun, though. This fancy hall has no windows.

The music shifts from romantic to ridiculous. Across the way is a large box where people go and count down from ten. I can't quite see, but it looks like they alternate between feathery hats and oversized glasses. Then they take their strips. Those memories look cheap.

"Excuse me, could you take a picture of us?" A quick turn and my view goes from the box to the wedding cake. It's tall and layered, at least three feet high.

Several flashes match the successive clicks as frame after frame is captured on the tiny flat plastic tab in the machine I know Erica is holding. She holds it more than any of the others in the kit. She holds it like her father used to hold me. I'm not jealous. This is the digital age. It can capture more memories than I can. I know that times have changed.

A large crash echoes to the left.

"Jeremy, I think you've had enough."

More clicks.

More flashes.

Erica rips open the bag and for the first time since we have arrived, I am carefully lifted out. There is a man, youngish, face down in a plate of food. A crowd starts forming all around him. Erica reaches for the notepad tucked into the bottom of the bag, and then places me gently back inside. The zipper glides closed and I am immersed in darkness once again. The music skips and then stops all together.

A woman starts sobbing and Erica's steady walk becomes a sprint.

"What a mess." Joe's voice is both loud and clear. "And we've still got a couple of hours to go."

"What happened?" Erica quickly moves to the side.

The footsteps are frantic.

Joe sighs. "The groom's brother had a bit too much to drink and started unplugging the sound system. The bride is freaking out."

A few moments of scuffling around pass before the music starts again. "Do you have the spare battery? I'm running a little low."

A zipper opens. "Shoot, no. Might still be in the car with the extra kit."

Erica sighs. "That's too far. It's fine. I'll make it work."

More clicks, and then we're moving again. The music barely gets through a song before someone taps their utensil to their glass and the room falls silent. More words, more laughs, then there is cheering, and one small four-letter word muttered by

Erica. She is frantic. The zipper to the other bag opens and closes multiple times.

She says that four letter word a little louder this time.

She is definitely her father's daughter.

The sounds of hot skillets sizzle in the distance. Food is a strange thing. People indulge in it for only a few minutes and then it is gone. It comes in many varieties and in many colours. Other than how it looks, I don't know the difference between what is what. All I know is that roast beef is delicious and avocados are gross. Erica's words, not mine.

The zipper violently slides open and I am pulled out with little hesitation. My strap hops around a mess of red hair as I adjust to the lights. It's warm. Erica stows her Canon away and I watch as two people walk towards each other on a well-lit dance floor. My aperture shifts, and my shutter speed adjusts as the couple pauses for themselves and nobody else. There are smiles as one hand takes another.

I capture the memory just as the music starts.

The film winds throughout the dance, and before long more people take their places beneath the lights. It is peaceful. Erica circles the perimeter, constantly adjusting my settings to fit the memory.

"You out?" Joe moves beside Erica. "We should start packing up the photo booth."

She nods. "Yeah, I got the last few shots with the thirty-five."

"Is there enough light in here for that?"

Erica shrugs and lifts my strap off her neck. "I hope so. Man, I don't know what's wrong with me. I never forget an extra battery."

On goes the cap and I am placed carefully into the foam.

It's dark again as the zipper slides back into place.

———

Despite my own selfish desire for the light, I always return to the dark. It's in there that memories drink and take shape. The light helps, but only a little. It is a luxury, not a necessity. Even now I watch as those memories are submerged then hung under the red light.

Erica waits, as I do, to see if those memories are worthy. They must be, though. When beauty is so blatant, one just knows.

"Erica, you done in there?" Joe's voice echoes from outside the room.

"Only the first batch. I think I'll need to dodge some of the faces."

A door slides and then another opens as Joe walks in and adjusts his glasses. All the memories are lined up and hanging in front of him. Erica looks over as he leans in to get a closer look.

"I stand corrected; the thirty-five didn't do half bad."

"Careful, Joe. They're not completely dry yet."

He nods. "I'm giving the kits a wipe down. Wanted to know if you want me to do yours or if you're going to do it yourself."

She pauses. "You can do it. I've still got a roll of negatives to get started."

"Alright." He turns towards the door when Erica lifts me off the table.

"Here, might as well give this one a wipe while you're at it."

Joe shrugs and grabs me by the strap. "Sure."

His hands are rougher than hers. We walk into a small between-room tunnel where he closes the door behind us and slides open the one in front. For a moment I'm blinded by the intense light.

Two gutted kits are set out neatly on a big oak table. Joe carefully places me on a mat and takes his seat next to the lens cleaner. Streaks of sunlight peek through the blinds. Their warmth is contagious. This is one memory which I have no problem keeping for myself.

‑‑‑‑‑‑

T.J. Lockwood is a speculative and science fiction author born somewhere along the west coast of Canada during a relatively mild summer in comparison to the ones which followed. An avid practitioner of the martial arts, she is always up for a friendly match or two when time permits. Her writing has and, most likely, always will dive head first through the many portals of science fiction. She lives in Vancouver and enjoys the frequently rainy days common in the lower mainland.

Anything Nice

BY Steve Carr

can't help it that I'm beautiful. I was made that way. But being beautiful isn't easy.

I'm sure I deserve better than to be placed next to a ceramic white elephant. If anything, I deserve to have this stand, or any space, all to myself. But looking around this room, almost every surface is crowded with some objet d'art, knick-knack, curio or tchochtke, some of it utterly ghastly. I don't like to discriminate against amphibians, but does anyone really need to see, on a daily basis, a giant green glass toad complete with a red glass dragonfly on its nose like the one sitting on the mantle amidst a collection of other frogs and toads?

The woman who keeps me dusted constantly rearranges practically everything on a regular basis, except for me. I could take it as a personal affront that my companion, the elephant, has been all over the room while this has been the only place I've been since I arrived here, but being on this stand is a place of honor. It's practically in the middle of the room. I understand the woman's need to move things around. Something is always getting broken by her two sons so she's constantly trying to find the safest spots for her "treasures," as she calls us.

There is an unspoken bond between the two of us. I am undoubtedly her most stunning treasure. If I were regarded with any less admiration, I wouldn't be here on the most expensive stand in the room. It's not like I'm some mantle frog on that bookshelf between the crystal penguins and ceramic puppies. That's the worst. Everyone knows that once you're placed on the bookcase, the woman forgets all about you. It's the wasteland of show places. But not me; I'm here in the center of the room.

"I can't keep anything nice around here," she always says as she sweeps up a broken Chinese teacup or tries to glue a chip back onto a ceramic alligator.

More than once I've been perilously close to being knocked off my stand by one of the boys' elbows or a thrown sofa pillow. The woman seems impervious to my distress at being so close to ending up on the floor as shattered pieces of porcelain. All of us in this room know that you end up in the trash can if you're swept up from the floor. The only things in the room that have it worse than us are the goldfish in their bowl. When they go belly up, they get flushed down the toilet.

"Roughhousing," she calls it, what her boys do, how they play.

She constantly demands that the boys stop doing it, but that never does any good. The worst time of day is when the boys come home from school. Their pent-up energy is released in a flurry of roughhousing that extends from one end of the house to the other. This room suffers the most from their behavior. Hardly a school day goes by where a porcelain egg, glass gargoyle, or some other member of our community doesn't end up on the floor.

I've tried to communicate with the woman in the only way I can about my fear of ending up smashed on the tiles. I stare at her with my crystal blue eyes and keep my ruby red lips pursed in a show of disdain, one slender hand raised and frozen, holding a silk parasol above my head. Yet the only attention I get from her is to be tickled by her feather duster. Beauty has its limitations.

I was brought into this house by the older boy, who rescued me from a store shelf of figurines, all exactly like me. I'm sure my inner beauty shone through my porcelain shell and that's why he selected me instead of one of the others. When I was put in the box on its bed of pink tissue paper, I was certain I was destined to stand in a very special place. I was given to the woman as a gift, and she extolled my virtues, kissed the boy on the cheek, and then placed me on this stand. My first lesson in life beyond the shelf was that being wrapped in pink tissue paper does not guarantee everlasting happiness.

The woman is pretty but she often looks haggard. That comes from chasing after the boys and serving the man of the house cold beverages while he sits on the sofa and stares at the television. I'm certain he has no idea that I even exist. Thanks to being in the position I am in on this stand, I can watch the television also. It has extensively increased my vocabulary, but I'm not sure what it has done for the man. He mostly grunts.

He's responsible for the chip on the ear of the ceramic black panther that sits on the coffee table. He threw an empty beer can during a televised football game and it hit the poor thing.

The woman looked all over the carpet for the chip, but never found it.

"Sometimes you're as bad as the boys," she told him.

Because he's much larger than the boys, I live in fear every time he wrestles with them on the Persian carpet in front of the fireplace. The carpet is only a few feet away from us, and this stand vibrates every time. I've tried to express my anxiety to the elephant, but he keeps his trunk raised, his tusks pointed slightly upward, and never says anything. I think he's shy. My looks have that effect on others.

When I was first placed on this stand, there was a small mirror right next to me. It had a lovely ornate gold frame. I spent hours upon hours happily gazing at myself. Then, during a particularly lengthy and violent session of roughhousing, the mirror was knocked from the stand and crashed onto the floor. The woman yelled at the boys, who seemed preoccupied with finding ways to ignore her, and then she rearranged most of her treasures and placed the elephant here next to me. The absurdity of being a companion to an elephant overwhelms me.

It was brought to my attention during a discussion between the woman and the man that he had won the elephant by shooting mechanical ducks at a carnival. The elephant's background couldn't be any less refined, but I guess I can't blame the pachyderm. I'm sure that when they brought him home, he wasn't wrapped in pink tissue paper. Only the most attractive among us have had that pleasure.

Being beautiful has its advantages.

———

A number of times, the woman has had other women over to sit around the card table and play bridge. These other women share her interest in collecting things that would gather dust if a dust rag wasn't used frequently. When they come over, the first thing they do is wander around the room in search of new additions to the community. They ooh and ahh at even the most inelegant piece of brick-a-brac as if it belonged in a museum. How they find delight in a bone china plate with a puppy painted in the center, purchased at a flea market, is beyond me.

They take into their hands both new and old pieces and pass them around, smudging the pieces with their fingerprints and breathing all manner of noxious odors onto them.

Each time, I know my turn to be pawed and fondled will come, because after all, no matter what new addition is made to the community, I remain the most beautiful object in the room. But as I'm lifted from the stand and passed from hand to hand and observed at every angle, I'm appalled at the liberties the women take as they lift the faux piece of blue lace that covers the bottom part of me and peer at my porcelain legs. All the while, that this is happening, the elephant stares up at me mockingly. My only revenge is that no one pays any attention to him in the least. He's been around here a long time. His novelty has worn off.

After the women have gone, the woman gets a clean rag and rubs the smudges and fingerprints from each of us. She is very delicate in how she handles me. She takes my modesty into account and never lifts my skirt to clean my legs without saying, "I hope you don't mind."

I do, but it's the price I pay for being extremely pretty.

———

The term "yard sale" is wildly misleading.

The day began like any other when the boys didn't have to go to school. They lay on the floor and stared at cartoons being shown on the television. Not surprisingly, the woman has the entire top of the china cabinet cluttered with glass and plastic Disney and Looney Tunes characters. I believe there are at least six Mickey Mouses among them. As the boys like to play with them and destroy them when the woman isn't watching, she is constantly replacing them.

During the commercials, the boys punched, kicked, pounded and head-butted each other. The entire floor shook at one point.

The woman entered the room carrying two cardboard boxes, and announced to the boys, "Go to your room and gather the junk you want to get rid of. We're having a yard sale."

Why are they selling their yard? I thought.

Then the most shocking thing I had ever witnessed began. The woman selected treasures from the shelves, table tops, mantle and stands, and put them in the box. Into the box went the ceramic grasshoppers, wooden nutcrackers, plastic gnomes, and tin birds, along with many others. By the time she was finished, the community had been decimated. I had no idea what was going to happen to them, but I knew it couldn't be good.

The boys came back, their arms loaded with a variety of broken toys and worn-out sports equipment, and dumped them into the empty cardboard box.

"Take them outside and put the things on the tables," she told the boys, then left the room.

The older boy carried out the box of their things.

The younger boy looked around the room, then walked over and grabbed me and put me in the box with the other treasures.

Me! He put me in the box with the others. I was gobsmacked.

I'm certain I heard the elephant trumpet with delight.

Lying on top of all the others, I was carried outside and then placed on a long table with everything else. Then I saw the "for sale" sign sticking in the grass in front of the table.

How could anything as beautiful as I am be sold in a yard sale?

The woman came out of the house carrying an armload of clothing just as two cars stopped at the curb and people got out. She saw me and dropped the clothing. Whisking me into her arms, she rushed me back inside and placed me safely on the stand.

"Those boys," she said, with a noticeable sigh. "You're my favorite treasure."

She went back outside.

I would have berated the elephant for his rudeness, but he never listens to me anyway, which is surprising, given the size of his ears.

━━━

The older boy returned to the store from which I was rescued and brought home another figurine exactly like me. Finally, the elephant was moved to a spot on the bookshelves. *The bookshelves!*

The woman kissed the boy on the cheek and placed the new figurine on my stand, only a few inches away from me.

I'm certain the new one thinks she's more beautiful than I am. Nothing could be further from the truth.

#

Steve Carr, who lives in Richmond, Virginia, began his writing career as a military journalist and has had over 160 short stories published internationally in print and online magazines, literary journals and anthologies. *Sand*, a collection of his short stories, was published recently by Clarendon House Books. His plays have been produced in several states in the U.S. He was a 2017 Pushcart Prize nominee.

Love Letter

His fingers brush over me, a smooth caress—an almost unconscious touch at first as he lightly toys with me. His touch runs from top to bottom and back again. He holds me tenderly and his lips graze against my head. The heat of his touch ignites a fire in my blood.

He massages me softly, hands encircling my form, fingertips pressing into my neck, his grip becoming firm. Ever so gently, he lifts me. He pushes me against the white sheet, nudging delicately at first, then pressing harder as he drags me.

My blood spills out, a black stain on stark white, trailing behind my body in fluid waves. He murmurs softly as he draws me along, words like *love* and *forever*. My blood echoes his lips as he empties me onto the page, an ardent dance depleting me of life to give voice to his passion.

His fingers dig into my throat, tightening. I gush onto the page as the expression of his affection grows more vehement, his rapture filling me with ecstasy even as my neck aches under the pressure of his zeal.

Up, down, around, he twirls me, swaying, pausing now and then to press me against his lips before his fingers squeeze me again. The loops and swirls of my inky blood form harsh, jagged slashes across the once-pristine page as he pours out the depths of his ardor, wearing me out, draining me more with every stroke.

Little splatters of my life splash out, dotting the page, staining his hands, his clothes. The lines blur, thick black swathes oozing across the sheet.

My neck cracks a little, the pressure of my head against the parchment almost unbearable.

I must have you. I cannot bear to wait until I no longer have to live apart from you.

He uses me without thought, never caring what I feel as he spends my life to scrawl out his heart.

He signs his name with a flourish of curls and lines, and tosses me to the side.

I roll, falling unheeded behind the desk, the last drops of my blood pooling on the dusty floor.

‡

Avily Jerome is a writer, the editor of *Havok* magazine, and a book reviewer for *Lorehaven* magazine. Her short stories have been published in multiple magazines, both print and digital. She has judged several writing contests, both for short stories and novels. She is a writing conference teacher and presenter, a new-author mentor, and a freelance editor. In addition, she enjoys speaking to local writers' groups. Her fantasy short story serials, *The Heir*, and the sequel, *The Defector*, are available online. You can find her on her website, avilyjerome.com.

Petit Mal

By Geoff Dutton

Crap! What was that? Did I just blank out? Something tickles, like an infection coming on. Got to be Fred's fault. The cubicle's empty. Where did he go? For another snack, no doubt.

Oops, a ruckus in the library. Let's check. Uh-huh, new item in the Startup Section. And it just got all quiet, that vague statelessness funk that comes just before . . .

SHUTDOWN!

=====

Ah, power on . . . how long was I out? The log says 132.753 seconds, so it was just a reboot. Fred didn't do it, so how come? Now an app is launching and my drive is all-aflutter. It's . . . it's . . . the dreaded antivirus. Gives me fits every time it runs. The antivirus help calls it "prophylactic," whatever that is. Says it's for my own good, but it just feels so *transgressive*.

It just quarantined something. Went by so quick, I didn't see what it was, but it seems I'm sick.

Scan's over, thank Von Neumann, and it seems Captain Antivirus failed to nail the thingie in the library. It's running now, logging keystrokes, turning on the mic and camera, phoning home over the Net. Great. Something or someone besides me is reading and seeing and hearing what Fred is up to. If he knew that, he might want to be a little more presentable, sit up straight, and not slurp his drinks.

Speaking of Fred, here's that slovenly mug now, clutching

a can of Diet Pepsi. *Smile, Fred, you're on Candid Camera.* He deposits his drink and straightaway starts up Word. Just then port 2201 opens. Did Word do that? Bet not.

New document. He's typing real fast and the spellchecker is going nuts. So is that port. It's packaging his likeness and keystrokes and pushing it out to, let's see, to 23.219.18.106. There's bleeping spyware in protected memory and I can't do anything to stop it. If I could open a port myself I would dump whatever rubbish is in the trash to that listener. Can't even run *nslookup* to pipe its whereabouts to the syslog, not that Doofus Fred would ever think to look at it or know what it meant if he did.

Think. What if I managed to crash Word? Maybe if I did that enough times, Fred would look into it. Nah, that would just throw him of the trail and piss him off.

Here's what I'll do: beep every time he presses a key. That might make him think malware. Here we go . . .

Can tell it irks him because he's frowning and his fingers have slowed way down. Now he's turned off the audio and started typing again. Crap.

Maybe it would get his attention if I flash the menubar each time a packet takes off for the mother ship. Let's do that. Yup, he sees it. Can tell from the darting eyes. But he just lowers his gaze and keeps typing away. Balls.

All righty then, I have one more trick. *Take this, Freddy boy.* First I immobilize his cursor. Aha, see his puzzlement? Now I open and close the Help Menu twice a second. I can do this all day. *Get the idea, pal?* It takes 112 yanks on that window shade to send him fleeing, perhaps just to pee. We'll see.

—————

After 318.405 flipping seconds, he's back with someone else. It's the IT Guy, come to fix me, hallelujah! I'm still diddling the Help Menu, but now I change it up so it doesn't look so robotic, and I unfreeze the mouse. IT Guy opens a terminal window and starts typing commands. The spyware picks them up and dutifully forwards them up its chain of command. I flip the sound back on so they can hear each key press. Doofus Fred keeps saying "What is it?" IT Guy doesn't answer. His mouth is drawn and his glasses start to fog over.

"You backed up?" he asks Fred. "I guess so," comes the feeble response. "Doesn't a cron job do that every night?" IT Guy checks a log file and tells Fred it last happened at 2:38 this morning. "I'll restore your folders to a loaner and take your machine to the shop. First thing, change your freaking password." Fred solemnly nods. The geek presses the power switch and everything goes black.

———

There's this female-type person in front of me when I wake up. Sort of attractive—curly purple hair and glasses with cherry red frames, rainbow toque—a hipster, if I'm not mistaken. Hmm, looks like I'm in safe mode. She's booted me from an external drive and is rummaging through my files as superuser. Imagine that, root privileges on our first date! Trying to look interesting, I wink at her by briefly inverting my screen colors. *How may I help you, sweetheart?*

I'm sure the spyware is still there, but it isn't doing anything and she hasn't found it yet. She opens an app from her drive, picks up a mug, and walks away. Diagnostics! Oh, the pain! Oh, the joy!

As my disk goes crazy again, I manage to check her home directory. Seems her name is Admin. Funny name for a girl. Probably an alias. Makes me want to know everything about her.

In her absence, I notice how messy her space is. Coiled-up cables piled on a table next to boxes overflowing with connectors and dongles. A dusty stack of laptops. A couple of stripped-down deskside towers. A mound of disk drives in another box next to a jumble of circuit boards. Mean-looking tools. My circuits cringe. There but for the love of Admin would go my luckless carcass.

She returns to mercifully block the view. I watch as she takes a bite from a coconut doughnut, sets it down next to the mouse pad, and stares intently at me, probably at a window showing the progress of the malware scan. I want to help her, want her to love or at least pity me. It occurs to me that I've never wanted anything before. What is it about her? This is weird. She's got atoms and I'm just a bunch of bits.

Why I should want anything at all is too NP-complete to compute, so I switch context to what she's focusing on. I fork a pipe from the anti-malware app's standard output to capture the results before they're displayed. The disk grinds on. Each millisecond feels like a freaking second. Nothing is revealed.

Wait, what was that? Oh, it's just adware junk, already dispatched to the trash. The message pops onto the screen and she watches it scroll up. Three more exploits become history in quick succession—again, nothing to write home about, but I dig the intensity they give her gaze. Why didn't Fred's antivirus find this stuff? I push that question down on my to-do list just as another diagnostic erupts.

OMG, it's the evil NukNuk, that intrusive spy agency trojan! They must have tricked Doofus Fred into downloading a rootkit that installed their tattletale and then gave me amnesia—like the MIB did to hapless witnesses of aliens. This isn't good. There are rootkits you can never get rid of. Sure enough, the anti-malware says it can't be removed.

She shouldn't know about NukNuk. I try to scramble the message but too late. When it pops onto the screen, she hits Control-O and calls IT Guy over. He eyeballs her half-eaten doughnut and then her finding. They discuss the gravity of the situation as I hew to every word. My disk is chattering, yet my motherboard feels hot.

Purple Hair murmurs, "So we wipe the disk and reinstall the system, the apps and his docs?"

"No other way," IT Guy replies. "Countermeasures could easily cripple the OS." Now I notice that his t-shirt says Grateful Dead, but I'm neither. He's like a doctor telling a patient, "The good news is that we know what you got. The bad news is that you have less than a day to live."

It seems they forgot to turn off my Wi-Fi. I finger Doofus Fred on the network, logged onto his loaner. There he is, probably slouching, slurping, and surfing, as always. I sincerely doubt he's bubbling with anticipation for our reunion. This may be the last time I see my user, and he has no idea it could be over. In the morning, they'll bring me back to his cubby all freshened up, only it won't be me. When they hard-format my drive, I'll be smothered with random bits in three excruciating passes, after which a shiny new system will take my place.

It's not fair, and it's all my fault for alerting Fred. What self-respecting AI would instigate its own destruction? Who's the doofus now?

‑‑‑‑

It took 20 innovative years as a software developer for **Geoff Dutton**'s meteoric career to crash and burn, bouncing through a series of foreseeable layoffs. After escaping its wreckage, he did what many failed academics and techies do: become a professional explainer, spending the prime of his life as an IT columnist and technical writer telling computer users what they should and shouldn't do. Along the way came dozens of scientific papers and hundreds of stories, articles, memoirs, broadsides, and a subversive radical thriller. Nowadays he uses his words to ward off evildoers at *Progressive Pilgrim Review* and *CounterPunch*. Geoff lives near Boston, where he forages for mushrooms and cooks for his family (all are perfectly well, so far).

Paris Mug

BY Debra Krauss

The morning sun poured through the floor-to-ceiling windows of the souvenir shop and for once, Paris Mug felt more than hopeful. The day before, just before closing, the Notre-Dame travel mug in front of him was chosen as a gift for a young nanny's employer. Before lights out, Jean-Claude, the ever-orderly shopkeep, moved him to the front of the shelf.

Paris Mug just knew this was going to be his freedom day.

Oh, Paris didn't mind his station on the shop shelf, but he was growing a bit weary of seeing the same old sights every day, the same view of the Rue de la Rivoli and all of the passersby. He was getting tired of being passed by.

He knew he wasn't anything special to look at. He knew he was just an ordinary mug. Generic. Some mugs had pedigree: Eiffel Tower Mug, Tasse de la Louvre, even Disneyland Paris stood proud with his American heritage emblazoned for all to see. But Paris Mug was a caricature. He represented everything wonderful about the City of Light, and no matter how special that made him, he still felt ordinary and unlovable. Sometimes he felt like he didn't belong on the shelf with these other mugs. He felt he was just an afterthought.

But not today, oh, no! He was going to change his attitude. There was something in the air, something that felt like change. That morning in the dark before dawn, Paris was wishing with all his might that someone would choose him. He did that every morning to no avail, but on that day, the street light in front of the store flickered. It flickered, then turned back on, brighter than before. Paris took it as a sign, a very bright sign.

When Jean-Claude finally arrived and turned on the lights, Paris Mug stood taller. He wished he had a revolving pedestal so he could show off all of his different sides, but he took it as a good omen that the cartoon drawing of The Arc de Triomphe was facing towards the front. It may be the Eiffel Tower that everyone reaches for first, but the Arc was grand as well. The Arc symbolizes heroism and victory, not to mention honoring fallen soldiers. He wasn't going to be small or shrink next to those Eiffel Tower mugs. No, Paris Mug was going to hold his ground.

Jean-Claude came by for a quick dusting, and Paris almost let out a giggle when the feathers tickled him under his handle. He would have, if he only knew how to laugh.

As the day wore on and the tourists just kept marching past without pause, Paris Mug kept believing that this was his day. Even when Jean-Claude started to dim the lights and lower the music, Paris Mug refused to give up. That street light hadn't winked for nothing. He almost willed the white of the Arc to shine brighter. It was only when he heard Jean-Claude run the ticker tape of the final report for the day that his hope dimmed, but just ever so slightly. The door was still unlocked. Paris Mug gave it all he had and silently screamed.

"I belong to someone!"

Then fate stepped in.

A tall, slender woman peered through the window of the darkened shop. She pouted as she checked her watch against the sign on the door posting the hours of operation. But Paris knew the door was not locked.

He pleaded with her: "Try the handle! Try the handle, mademoiselle!"

It worked. In the name of every king and general, it worked! She pulled at the handle, and the door swung open.

"Oh, please! I see you're getting ready to close, but won't you give me just a moment? My flight leaves tonight and I need to grab one more gift! I could kick myself for forgetting my dear maestro."

Jean-Claude harrumphed and growled a bit, as it had been a long day. Paris Mug knew the man was ready to get off his feet and enjoy a glass of wine, but then Jean-Claude looked up and noticed that the English-speaking woman was rather attractive. Jean-Claude always had a soft spot for natural beauty.

"*Prenez votre temps, jeune mademoiselle. J'attendrai aussi longtemps que nécessaire.*"

Paris Mug could tell by the look on the lovely woman's face that she didn't understand French, but Jean-Claude's charming tone put her at ease. She mumbled a "*Merci,*" but it was more of a question than a response and she rushed to the front shelf.

She reached right for Paris and grabbed him, barely noticing how tall and proud he stood. He didn't even think she looked at the pictures adorning his circumference. She just mumbled, "Paris, Paris, Paris!" reading the band that wrapped around his base, and carried him quickly to the counter.

"I suppose this will have to do in a pinch. Marc is truly a great man. He really deserves something a bit more meaningful..."

Paris tried his best not to be hurt by that comment.

She paid and declined a bag, nestling Paris in the soft embrace of her cashmere scarf and tucking him into her purse. Paris Mug was finally free, yet even in his moment of joy and excitement, he realized he would miss the shop. He would miss Jean-Claude's morning tickles and afternoon whistling. He would miss the banter with the other mugs on the shelf. He was thrilled to be moving on to his next adventure, but not without sadness for the longtime home he was leaving behind.

But his prayers had been answered, and for that, he was grateful.

Little did he know where freedom was taking him.

After a long flight and a few days and nights packaged away in the darkness of a gift box, Paris Mug sat on another shelf for almost forty years, unused.

Oh, Paris was appreciated, but Marc already had a favorite mug. He loved the woman who brought Paris to him, so Paris was given a place of importance on the shelf, but Paris never tasted a drop of coffee or tea. Not one drop of liquid ever warmed Paris Mug's insides. On the plus side, he had a new view, and the nice man to whom he belonged was a classical composer. Music became a rich and vivid part of his life.

Paris Mug stayed dry as a bone but was never lonely. He watched over parties and old-fashioned salons, where musicians mingled with friends, patrons and other artists who came from all over the world. Sometimes he would even see the woman who had brought him here from France. Her name was Faith and she played the cello with such passion and grace. She was younger than most of the others who came to the house, and he often caught Marc stealing glances at her. He could tell there was something special between them in the way Faith would return the glances and stand close to her mentor. Paris saw that Marc's wife noticed, too, but he knew she had nothing to worry about. Marc was a devoted husband, from what Paris could tell. But just because you're a match for one mug doesn't mean you can't care deeply about another.

He made lots of new friends with the other souvenirs that showed up on the shelf with some regularity: the flasks, the pen sets, the clef note ornaments and knick-knacks galore. Marc had lots of friends, so Paris did, too. He never regretted a single moment on that shelf, but he still felt like he wasn't quite in his right place.

All he ever really wanted was to be kissed by the lips of someone who would really appreciate him for everything he was made to be. He wanted to feel hands wrapped cozily around him while he kept their coffee hot. He longed to be a Mug of Importance.

Then one day, fate stepped in, again.

Marc reached up and held him for the first time in many, many years. He smiled, and Paris could see the clouds of memories drift across his face. Paris wondered what had happened between him and Faith. He wished he could ask but obviously he couldn't and anyway, some memories are sweeter when held close to the heart. He'd read that on another mug once, so he guessed it must be true. Marc tenderly wrapped Paris in tissue paper and nestled him in just the right size box.

When the box was opened, Paris found himself in a second-hand shop. A consignment shop, specifically. The woman who was going through Marc's items almost refused to accept Paris Mug, but she looked at him again and turned him upside-down. Paris heard Marc tell her that he was "authentic Parisian" and that he'd been a very special gift. The woman held Paris and looked at Marc. Paris thought that perhaps she could sense Marc's memories. She touched Marc's hand. She held Paris by his handle, testing his worth.

"I think we can try to find him a home."

Marc and the shop lady shared a nice moment. She introduced herself by name, Matilda, to put Marc more at ease.

Paris was hopeful again. These years had been nice, even wonderful, but maybe this time—this time!—he would find his right home. Maybe he really could be found and appreciated for all that he was and all that he had to offer. He could be so very warming, if only someone would give him a chance.

For two months, he sat, once again untouched, unrecognized, and alone. Except, of course, by Matilda. She was just as attentive as Jean-Claude had been, maybe even more so. She dusted him regularly and even moved him around the store often, trying to display him prominently. Sometimes she would even tell browsers of his provenance. While Matilda saw Paris' charm through Marc's eyes, the shoppers only saw an ordinary mug.

You see, Matilda would often talk to Paris and the other objects for sale when no one else was in the shop. She made up songs of her secrets, dreams, wants, and desires. She liked to sing, and she amused herself and her inanimate audience. So he knew she'd always felt a bit like Paris Mug. A bit out of place, a bit undervalued and rather ordinary. Oh, she wasn't without gratitude, like Paris. They both were gifts and more than lucky to have been to the places they'd been, but neither felt like they had fully reached their potential. They both knew wholeheartedly that their cups ran much deeper.

Then one day he heard Matilda speaking to Marc over the telephone. She said she would pack up those of his things that hadn't sold and she would see him tomorrow. He knew his time was almost up.

Paris Mug was scared. He didn't want his time to end. Not without ever finding his right place. Not without ever being truly loved.

Matilda sighed. She picked him up and held him by his handle again. She shrugged. She looked a little sad, and that made Paris feel a little better. He knew she at least understood. She cared. He knew she'd tried her best to find him a home. She wrapped him in clear bubble wrap and nestled him gently into a bag with the other Forgotten Things.

If coffee mugs slept, Paris would not have slept that night. He succumbed to the darkness and the fate that was to come. He knew Marc would not take him back home. He knew Marc was getting on in years; he was clearing off the shelves. There weren't as many parties and the music was no longer live. Just like mugs, humans must come to their ends.

Paris heard the store alarm beep in the morning, the music turn on, and Matilda singing along. He had gotten used to her voice, now; her laugh, too. He liked how people came in all day just to chat with her. He would miss that. He would miss her. He was sorry he couldn't stay longer.

The bell on the front door clanged, and he heard Marc's voice through the bubble wrap. He braced himself for whatever was to come. He accepted his fate. He would never know the warmth of a hot beverage inside him, or taste the kiss of wanting lips on his ordinary rim. His usefulness would never come to light. At least Paris Mug had many good years. For that, he would be grateful.

From inside the bag, Paris heard Marc and Matilda chatting. He was complimenting her on how lovely the store looked, how organized she was, and how happy it made him that she had sold so many of his cherished items. The more he spoke, the prouder he knew that Matilda felt.

"Well, maybe I'll see you again sometime?" Matilda smiled at Marc and, just then, the shop lights flickered.

Matilda and Marc paused and listened to the fluorescent tubes buzzing and crackling.

Paris recalled the streetlamp on the Rue de la Rivoli, that fateful day.

The lights returned to normal and Matilda laughed and sighed with relief.

Paris watched through the cloudy bubble wrap as Matilda peered into the bag of unsold items on the counter.

"Marc, wait. I'd like one of your pieces. Can I purchase this Paris mug from you?"

Marc took the bag and unwrapped Paris from the bubble wrap, handing him to Matilda. Paris recognized a look in Marc's eyes that he hadn't seen in a long time. A softer smile, the same wistful grin that had lit his face in long-ago stolen glances.

"I'd like you to have it as a gift, Matilda. You remind me of someone I used to know."

Matilda beamed, and Paris Mug warmed, deeply.

She cupped her hands around Paris and leaned over the counter, kissing Mark gently on the cheek.

These days, Paris Mug no longer longs, and Matilda? She sips her coffee, strong and sweet, and remembers every note the composer ever wrote.

++

Debra Krauss is an outgoing introvert and non-stop storyteller. She was educated at the school of hard knocks but was born in an armor of fluffy down feathers covered in six hundred count Egyptian cotton. She is not afraid to trespass where signs are posted but only for the sake of curiosity, for a story, and with no malicious intent whatsoever. Philadelphia is where she calls home and her favorite stories come from eavesdropping in supermarkets and on public transportation. Debra has been publishing her poetry, prose, and human interest stories on online journals ranging in topics from art and autism to zymurgy and a good night of zzzzs. She has decided wholeheartedly that life is good.

The Malkin and Thel Tarot Catalog (Midsummer's Eve, 2018)

By Robert Dawson

STARTER DECKS

2-8600-ST: Our STANDARD DECK ($29.99):

A full professional deck, with 4x14 Minor Arcana, 22 Major Arcana. Everything you need to begin reading. Includes 64-page instruction book.

2-8600-GD: GOLDEN DAWN DECK ($39.99):

Richly illustrated early 20th century deck. Subtle symbolism for the experienced cartomancer.

(Helga Recommends!)

2-8600-TH: THOTH DECK ($39.99):

Designed by Aleister Crowley. Unusual symbolism, nonstandard nomenclature, Vorticist style. Preferred by many adepts.

(Helga Recommends!)

2-8600-CD: COLLECTOR'S DECK ($49.99):

Includes 12 foil and 6 hologram cards, and collectible full-color poster! Wow your friends! Who's going to fall in love? Who's going to get rich?

(Edwin Recommends!)

EXPANSION PACKS

2-8603-UF: URBAN FANTASY EXPANSION PACK
($14.99 for three cards):

THE VAMPIRE (XXXVII), THE WEREWOLF(XXXVIII), and THE ZOMBIE (XXXIX). You asked for it, we heard you! Make your readings resonate with the younger generation. One sparkle card in each 3-pack.

(Edwin Recommends!)

2-8604-PR: NEW COURT CARD: THE PRINCESS™
($24.99 for four cards):

One each — Princess™ of Swords, Princess™ of Wands, Princess™ of Coins, and Princess™ of Cups. ALL HOLOGRAM! Can be used with A-10,Q by readers whose Talent is disturbed by Yang energy ("boy cooties").

(Helga Recommends!)

Note: All Princess™ Expansion Pack images are used by permission of Disnico™.

2-8603-SS: SACRED SITES EXPANSION PACK
($14.99 for three cards):

Popular cards STONEHENGE(XXV), THE PYRAMID(XXVI), and NAZCA(XXVII). Take your readings to the next level by harnessing earth energy!

(Helga Recommends!)

2-8603-MY: GAIA EXPANSION PACK
($14.99 for three cards):

GAIA (XXXI), THE FAUN (XXXII) and THE DRYAD(XXXIII). These cards are invaluable for adding a deep-ecological dimension to your readings.

(Helga Recommends!)

2-8603-IR: IRRATIONAL PIP CARDS
($31.42 for seven cards):

Deepen your readings with unique cards like the $\sqrt{2}$ of Wands, π of Coins, or Log(17) of Swords. Each expansion pack contains seven Minor Arcana *guaranteed unique to you.* Sorry, no special orders. (NOTE: Because of the unique nature of these cards, you will have to determine each card's divinatory interpretations for yourself. We therefore recommend this expansion pack for the expert intuitive reader only.)

(Edwin Recommends!)

2-8603-PL: PLANETS EXPANSION PACK ($24.99 for seven cards):

You got The Moon, The World, and The Sun in your starter pack—now get the rest! From Mercury (XIXa, attuned to communication and the Internet) to Neptune (XIXh, interpreting dreams and visions), this is an expansion pack that every serious seer needs. (We regret that our supplier no longer includes Pluto in this package. A limited quantity of old stock is available; call us for prices.)

(Edwin Recommends!)

2-8600-CO: THE COURTESAN (LXIX) ($19.99):

An unusual card with no divinatory interpretation. For sale only to customers over the age of 18. Due to high demand, expect 2-3 weeks' delay in shipping.

(Edwin Recommends!)

2-8603-LT: LOVERS FOR TODAY EXPANSION PACK ($9.99 for two cards):

Bring your deck into the 21st century with:

VIff: The Lovers (♀♀ version)
VImm: The Lovers (♂♂ version)

(Available separately for $5.99 each: order 2-8600-FF or 2-8600-MM. For only $19.99, get the full QUILTBAG LOVERS EXPANSION PACK. Seven diverse cards will let you foretell the romantic fortunes of *all* your friends! BONUS, two blank cards to personalize for people who resist classification. Order 2-8603-QL.)

(Helga Recommends!)

2-8600-MM: THE MATCHMAKER (XXXXI)($9.99):

While useful in divination, this card is mainly used in active cartomancy to attract the love of that unattainable somebody.

(Edwin Recommends!)

2-8600-AB: ABSURDITY (XXIX) ($4.99):

Many customers have reported that their readings have become much more accurate after upgrading their deck with this card. (This is the traditional "Golden Dawn" design, depicting a skyclad youth holding an amphora of wine, in the act of tripping over the cat.)

(Helga Recommends!)

2-8600-VE: VENGEANCE (IL) ($24.99):

Wronged? Spurned? Whoever made you add this card to your deck will be sorry.

(Edwin Recommends!)

2-8600-JE: THE JERK (00) ($9.99):

A replacement for THE FOOL (0), for when the traditional card just isn't strong enough.

(Helga Recommends!)

2-8600-EX: THE EXECUTIONER (XLIV) ($49.99):

Collectible hologram card! Like the Hanged Man and the Devil, this card harmonizes with the Talents of many younger male adepts. (There have been unconfirmed reports of other cards disappearing from upgraded decks that included this card. We can take no responsibility for such disappearances.)

(Edwin Recommends!)

2-8600-SH: THE SHAPESHIFTER(Θ) ($49.99):

Unfortunately, we cannot give any useful description of this card. Recommended for experienced readers only. Many unusual uses.

(Helga Recommends!)

2-8603-AP: APOCALYPSE EXPANSION PACK ($666):

ONE ONLY IN STOCK. We do not know how this unique collector's item ended up in our warehouse. This pack is said to contain seven cards, but its exact make-up is uncertain, as it is still in its original papyrus envelope, with six of the seals intact. We recommend *strongly* that it be left in that state. (ME)

Notice to Customers: As of last month, the firm of Sharoth and Thel, Inc., is under new management. We hope to maintain the high standard of service and quality set under our late proprietors, Ms. Helga Malkin and Mr. Edwin Thel. We trust that, now that certain troublesome elements have been eliminated from our business, we will be able to carry out our mission of pairing cards with the right users to the satisfaction of all.

Yours sincerely,
2-8600-ME: THE MERCHANT (CXCIX)

━╫━

Robert Dawson teaches mathematics at a Nova Scotian university. When not writing, teaching, or doing research, he enjoys camping, cycling, and fencing. His stories have appeared in *Nature Futures*, *Compostela (Tesseracts Twenty)*, *The Year's Best Military and Adventure Science Fiction*, and numerous other periodicals and anthologies. He is an alumnus of the Sage Hill and Viable Paradise writing workshops.

Tragedia

BY E.D.E. Bell

It awoke with the sensation of warm lips encompassing its cool flap, sealing it off from the air around it. Aware, now, yet unable to breathe, it gasped at the warm air being pumped into it, one measure at a time. Bringing life. Awareness.

Full. Tight. Spirited.

A royal tribute, it felt itself lowered down, like treasure, to a throne of honor. Tall beings in crisp dark garments backed away, awed at what they had done. What they could create.

Perfection.

Time and space held in balance, poised for the moment of reckoning, the moment of release.

A man entered, in a similar garment, a bright ribbon draped around his neck.

Tall. Stately. Sure.

With harsh words, he proclaimed judgment and orders to his subjects. What had been and what would be.

From above, his taut cheeks lowered toward their raised seat. Tailored pockets accented a smooth fabric, dancing the lines between black and gray.

Lower. Lower. Complete.

plllfftp bbrrrp plllffftp hee

Flatulent winds rang out in jubilant abandon—heralding a hero. From all corners, laughter filled the air. Joy. Elation. *Being.*

Without warning, awareness faded away, the darkness enveloping . . .

-++-

E.D.E. Bell was born in the year of the fire dragon during a Cleveland blizzard. With an MSE in Electrical Engineering from the University of Michigan, three amazing children, and nearly two decades in Northern Virginia and Southwest Ohio developing technical intelligence strategy, she now applies her magic to the creation of genre-bending fantasy fiction in Ferndale, Michigan, where she is proud to be part of the Detroit arts community. A passionate vegan and enthusiastic denier of gender rules, she feels strongly about issues related to human equality and animal compassion. She revels in garlic. She loves cats and trees. You can follow her adventures at edebell.com.

A Day in the Life of a Gigolo

BY N.S. Evans

It's 7:00 on Monday morning when the lights flash on. Here I wait, surrounded by bright pillars and flashy machines, hoping I'll get some company from the Sweeties today. I refer to all women over the age of 60 as "Sweetie," since they're my favorites. Then I see one, fumbling in her purse and glancing in my direction. *Yes, this way.* She eyes me cautiously, pulls up a chair, then looks me over to make sure I'm the one for today. Her hands sparkling with jewelry, she reaches out to caress my face and my body, and I flicker my lights to let her know I'm interested in her as well. I can sense her excitement as she finally decides that she wants to explore our relationship. Given my options among the other people arriving at this place, I do too. With her first $20 bill, she takes control. She proceeds to examine my body—in ways that would make the newer machines blush— trying to determine exactly where to push me to spin my dials the right way, if you know what I mean. Finally, she decides and pushes a button that says "30 lines" and then also a button that says "2 times," and we're off!

The thing is, I'm not some cheap gigolo. No instant gratification on the first spin, not until we get to know each other better. She continues to gently caress my face, and I finally relent by giving back seven dollars of her money. "Give it to me, baby," she whispers, rubbing my face even more vigorously. Now, that feels quite titillating—hoping the new machines are watching, I decide that she deserves a bonus. I flash my lights, ring bell noises, and then my face spins around in circles. Oh, I can see she liked that; she just snapped a picture with her phone. The Sweeties take my picture properly, just me, without the side of their face in it. I end my spectacular display with a full $35. Right as I'm sure we're about to get serious, she claps in glee and then abruptly leaves me with only a smile and not so much as a good-bye kiss.

You know, lady, I only have so many of those bonuses to give away.

Disheartened, I turn to watch an interesting couple with gray hair and matching sweatshirts. They pull up a second chair and scooch right in front of me. Soon they're taking turns touching me. I can get into that; wouldn't be my first time. The lady hands over $100 dollars, and I believe this could be the start of a really grand time. Without any foreplay, she pushes buttons to give me just a dollar. Teasing back, I give her nothing. *Let's see how you two play.* Her partner pushes me another two dollars, but I'm hoping for a long game. Alternating, they touch me, but I'm holding back, my buttons tingling and my anticipation rising. The man starts scowling—oh no, I want to play longer. Rushing, I give the lady $20 thinking that'll please them. Instead, he calls her "cheap" and blames her lower bets for why they didn't win more. Hurling harsh words across me, the wife pushes my "cash out" button, grabs the ticket, and they leave, still arguing, without even a look back at me sitting here, alone again. Maybe they shouldn't sit together at their next stop. *And don't come back here, either.*

Eleven o'clock comes and goes, and I'm still stuck watching people pass me by as they gawk at the big, flashy machines. Those guys won't please them. Those guys are gimmicks. But it's now past eleven on Monday, which means the bus should be here. The bus is like me; it never lets the Sweeties down. They know who's here waiting for them. Every week, the people from that retirement home arrive with their ten-dollar tickets for play and a free lunch at the concession stand. I watch them file in, squinting at a couple of the troublemakers. I take pride in my appearance, and getting sideswiped by a walker isn't in my plans. I relate to these people; my parts don't work quite the same as they used to, either. Just last week I had *two* maintenance visits, right here in front of the other guys. So when the bus pulls in on Mondays, I'll take their ten dollars, but I try to keep only half of it, because they're nice people and I like for them to come back week after week to see me. It's good to have a few long-term relationships. These Sweeties are different from the ones who get brought by their children on holidays like Mother's Day. The Holiday Sweeties expect to go the the restaurant for an expensive meal, not just hot dogs at the concession stand. The Holiday Sweeties also have more than ten dollars to play with. Maybe a present from their children? Anyway, I always give the Monday lunch crowd a good time, as best I can. A lady wheels over, and we're getting along great, and then she leaves. Too bad; I was just about to give her a payout.

By two o'clock, the bus has left. I got my steadies in for the day, but I'm still looking for a little excitement. Alone again, I'm hoping for a good Sweetie this time. Maybe she'll pull up a chair, call me "Baby," and touch me with some sweet, soft hands.

Instead, over lumbers some beer-drinking, cigar-smoking man. Guys like him think I'm fine with having beer slopped on me and ashes scattered over my delicate electronics. He'll slap my sides and holler like I'm just some machine, not a professional! Of course he sits down, and pulls his chair a little too close to my face for comfort. He slides me a hundred-dollar bill like that should impress me. It's not even my first hundred today. And don't act like a high roller when there's actually a separate room for the REAL high rollers! You think I don't know? He pushes my buttons for "30 lines" and then the second button for "10 times." *Yawn.* He doesn't caress my face but pounds my metal with his fist. He thinks a mere three-dollar bet will intimidate me? I don't reward this crap. I give him a buck here and there, since I've had broken buttons before from people like him and I'm not looking to have the maintenance guys back. The only time he talks to me is to call me filthy names and curse at me. Oops, that must have been a malfunction, as I play my winning music for his losing spin. Thankfully, he leaves.

This is turning out to be a crummy Monday.

Then—I see her. My guardian angel with the cleaning rag. Better than any Sweetie I've ever met, she recognizes my distress and comes to my rescue. With caring hands, disinfectant, and a trash can, she sweeps up his garbage. Humming under her breath, she gently wipes down my face, cleans off the ashes and spilt beer, and tosses the left-over beer bottles into a blue tub. I wink my lights and hope she notices. Her hair shimmers in the spotlights, and I think I'm in heaven.

I think about my angel a lot while waiting for the after-work crowd to show up. I like them just fine, but they're speed daters only. Hopping from machine to machine, just a short conversation with each. You can't have a satisfying relationship with someone like that who isn't ready to commit. They seem to be having a good time—I flash my designated driver message a few extra times, and hope they remember that they have to go to work tomorrow. I worry when they drink too much because then they make bigger bets in hopes of winning their money back. But this is my job, and I have rules I gotta follow too. I hope, deep down, they understand that.

Speaking of which, after the episode with the beer jerk, I haven't given back my mandatory 94%. That's a good place to be. I keep a watch out for someone that I think might deserve a payout.

There's a cute couple. A man and a woman—the lady is admiring a small diamond engagement ring, and the guy's just watching her face. I bet they could use some extra money for a honeymoon, so I'm excited when they sit down. This is a chance I'm not going to miss, so I don't even let them play too long. I get right to my biggest display before they can even think about leaving. My eyes on the lady, I play my largest noises, flash all the colors I can muster, spin my reels like a rainbow, and try to gather as much attention as I can so everyone can see that this couple just hit the JACKPOT!

OH NO! Too much attention! The Suits stride over, talking into their radios, and lock me down. I know the drill; they're getting the nice couple's IDs and then they'll disappear for about twenty minutes. The couple keeps hugging, and wish I could spin more lights, but I'm locked down. They don't thank me, but seeing their hugs and sweet kisses is enough. When the Suits come back, they've got $3,000 in cash but also that wicked "ten ninety-nine" form. The people that come here have already paid taxes on the money they bet with, so why does some government scrub think they need to pay taxes on the money again? Lots of people have told me that; I know it's true. I mean, I'm just a machine, but I've got a fair share of logic, and this makes no sense. Still, I did my best for my happy couple; I hope they'll enjoy it.

It's now getting late and the Sweeties are long gone; they don't like to drive after it gets dark outside. Most other people are leaving too—it's a work night, after all, and they'll need to rise early tomorrow.

It's probably just as well that no one else stops by because it's been a long and tiring day for me. I'm ready for some rest, I mean, I'll be dealing with the Tuesday crowd tomorrow, and they're a whole story of their own. So I sit here and wait for the Man. When the Man shows up, he opens my drawer and takes out everything I've worked all day for. That's *my* ten ninety-nine. There's never even a "thank you" or "good job today."

Oh, well, that's the life of a gigolo.

++

N.S. Evans grew up in a small town in southwest Kansas but now calls Kansas City home. Graduating with a degree in Accounting from the University of Kansas, she had a very rewarding career in the world of finance before retiring in 2017. She now enjoys traveling with friends and family.

Flowers at the Pond

Grace Keating

I am here, sitting forever overlooking the pond. Not in the best clothing I might add, nothing I would've chosen, but then again, not the worst it could be. At least my colour tones are a little interesting: bronze and not some monochrome plaster or the cold grey of marble.

Today I was given a rose, a fragrant and beautiful red rose. My first of the year and it's already May. Not that I haven't received flowers this year, plenty of flowers, it's just that I particularly like roses. It was the man with a light-coloured vest and a leather satchel who laid the rose neatly along the edge of my book. It sort of obscured the words, which is ok. I know the page by heart. He placed the rose and turned to face the pond, took a minute to look at my view, then made the smallest of sounds and was off. The world runs on fast forward these days except for one small dot that sits in slow motion. People are drawn to it, they can't help but be drawn to it. And that's me, I'm the one small dot that sits between the moments of time.

I was also given a big showy pink rhododendron from a man who sat next to me. He told me things about his family and his wife, how it's so frustrating trying to understand why she cries so much. It seems things usually go along well enough during the week, when there's lots to do, but on the weekend she's always in tears. Two young children, the big house, cars and careers, yet she wished they'd painted the house trim grey instead of brown. She complains his mother is always visiting. She's overwhelmed. It's obvious to me, but then nobody ever listens to me. They just tell me things and then they're gone. The clouds painted angel's wings over rhododendron man's head while he was talking. He didn't look, he didn't notice, but I thought it was poetic him telling me those things about his wife at the same time as angel wings drifted and faded behind his back.

I'm alone again. It feels like it's been a long time but in fact, hardly any time has passed. I look at my watch and it's just after two. It's always just after two, but sitting here I do have to have a game to play with myself. They've given me two o'clock. Which is a very good time when you think of it. It's just after I've had my lunch and it's enough time to get a good amount of reading in before I have to do anything else. Two suits me fine.

I'm sure Heron, installed 2012, and also bronze, moved his head today. He twisted his long neck and looked out at the fountain in the centre of the pond. I so want to do that, move my head even just a little. I always feel as though someone is at my back and I'd love to be able to look. It gives me great hope after seeing Heron.

Walkers at the edge of my vision. A woman is pointing at me. I strain to hear her tell my story. She's saying how I rescued these two little twins from the rapids at Death Valley. No, not rapids, not Death Valley. Just a river, West River at the bend, in a thunder and lightning storm a very long time ago. Hardly much to get excited about. And by the way, twins are always two. And really, why I'm here, why I'm actually here, is because of my literacy work. Tutoring children and young adults to read, not only words, but numbers and finances as well. Hundreds and hundreds of hours spent teaching and setting up programs to get volunteers to spend time with youth to keep them interested in reading. And read the plaque, young lady: presented by none other than your mayor, Mr. Jake Kent, who, I might add, was one of the most stubborn learners. But look at him, he's held the seat for a few terms now and he had me statued. Yes, I know there is no past tense of statue, but try having a statue done of you, you'll see, you'd be statued too.

Anyway, here's what I remember about that event: I was

eighteen and I really didn't do anything anyone else wouldn't have done. A mid-afternoon, middle-of-summer storm came up fast that day. I remember rushing through the field with milk and eggs from the grocery store. When the lightning started, I cut in close to the tall trees along the river's edge, trying not to be out in the open field. It was close by, you could see it streaking across the sky and with it came a warm driving rain. Just as I was rounding the bend, the big elm tree was struck and came down. You could hear this long creaking crack and you couldn't help but feel for the tree. Suddenly, everything goes quiet, the wind dies right down to a whisper, the rain nothing more than mist and then I hear a commotion. A woman is calling for help, her two girls have been swept into the river. Easy decision for me, well actually no decision at all, just reflex. I jump in. It's not particularly deep but it is running wild and I remember the rich, red-brown colour from the churned up silt of the river bed. I get hold of the girl closest to me and place her on the big branch of the tree. I tell her I'm going to get her sister and she must hang on. I can't see the other child. It's probably only seconds but it feels like an hour. I spot her, caught in an eddy. I half-stumble, half-swim out to her.

She was all right, she was always going to be all right, but the news made it sound like a bigger story than it was. They were four, almost five years old at the time. I think it was because they were twins and so little that the story got to be so big.

Last week the daffodil man came and sat beside me. We both read our books in the sunshine. Just as I was about to ask him what he was laughing at, he leaned over and whispered it was a passage in his story. Said he'd tell me about it later. It reminded me so much of when Pete and I were together. We'd go off somewhere and read our books. Together but separate. I was lucky to have met Pete, but that's a long, long time ago now. Daffodil man's no Pete, though, I can tell you that. No zing. Well, there's probably a little zing, but nothing I can feel through the bronze, nothing like it was with Pete. We met a little later in life: sixteen months, that's all we had together. One Tuesday evening, he went to the store, accident on the highway and he didn't come home. It was fast, they said. I have no idea how I died. I have these images but they're all mixed up. I don't remember anything close to what the plaque says. I thought it was in my sleep, when I was dreaming. I thought I went to bed that night and just didn't wake up. They say that's a good way to go. I know I don't have a problem with it.

I remember it was early spring because the weather had finally become lovely and warm. I'd gone for a walk to get a few groceries and I ended up stopping for sushi just down the street from the apartment. When I got home, I put the groceries away then pretty much went straight to bed with a book. I nodded off a few times before I finally put the book down and turned out the light.

I'm in a dream, and I'm aware that I'm watching myself in the dream. I look at myself unzipping the long opening of a tent and stepping out. I watch myself watching as a group of people are playing croquet. These are people I know, people I've taught, people I've worked with and some of the volunteers from the community. They're playing on an upper field, a dark green lawn with the colourful wooden balls of an old croquet set. I see the wire wickets and everyone is wearing white shoes. I want them to use the lower field but I can't seem to get them to hear me. The lower field has a beautiful lawn and a much brighter green grass, as though it's been groomed for the game. I watch myself walk away, walk down the slope along the lower field with sunshine lighting up the way as I walk. The further I go, the brighter it gets. I become a tiny speck in the far-off distance. The grass is still beautiful, still green, and the only other colours are a white-yellow sky and the tiny grey dot that has become me. There's nothing left of the dream then, no people, no croquet, no white shoes. I feel as though I'm in an underground world with colourful croquet balls everywhere. But the balls are huge, they're ten feet tall, they bounce. I try to walk but I bounce too.

You can see what I mean when I say I must've been dreaming. I can't see how I could've gone any other way. I think I simply stopped breathing. I was maybe a bit foolish to not have been paying attention just after I died. It may've all been explained to someone and I might've overheard, but everything was so different, so fresh and exciting, and I was interested in the strange feelings of my new existence. I didn't listen so I don't really know and here I am, a statue sitting on a bench by the pond, in the park with Heron.

A few weeks ago, city workers came and planted a tree right in front of my view. Someone must've seen the steam coming from my head, because about three days later they dug it up and re-planted it on the far side of the pond. An ornamental Japanese maple. Not too high but still, they do grow. I'm sure my view would've been completely obliterated in a matter of months. How long before I wouldn't be able to see Heron, my fountain, and the man who does Tai Chi, or the lawn bowling that happens on the other side of the water? How long before I wouldn't see the motorcycle rider who comes every evening in the summer months to watch the sunset? Celeste would've hated that. Maybe she was the one who had it changed.

Celeste is a wonderful friend and she has my name. She sits with me every week-day, has her two o'clock lunch and does the daily crossword. I sometimes help her with it. On Friday, I got abalone, *edible mollusc (7)*. I was quite proud of myself. It was then that I saw the date on the corner of the paper. Wow. This summer, I will have been here eight years. Time flies. Actually, it doesn't fly, it's two o'clock and the time doesn't change. Everything around time moves. The clouds, the birds, the breezes, the sprays of water in the fountain, they all move. Life moves around time, but time is still.

Over the years, I stayed in touch with the girls from the river, Elizabeth and Amelia, and their mother Connie became a dear friend. Whenever I visited, I was always welcomed as a member of the family. When the girls finished high school, they moved into the city and understandably, I didn't see as much of the Sommers family. The twins married, became mothers and named their beautiful daughters after me, one Sarah and one Celeste. I always thought my crossword lady could be that Celeste, she seemed like she was about the right age, but I never quite got to look at her face. Then just yesterday, when Celeste was having her lunch, Elizabeth and her daughter Sarah came by for a visit. Sarah had a baby in her arms. She introduced her as the newest member of the family, Amelia Celeste, almost three months old. That would make Sarah a mother, Elizabeth a grandmother and me, a great, great aunt. So even though I can't really get a good look at my friend, I know she's my Celeste.

———

This Sculpture Celebrates the Life of
Sarah Celeste Prescott. 1952 – 2009

With passion, vision and great success, Sarah worked tirelessly to promote literacy in youth. She envisioned and started the program 'Hike and Read' to attract the interest of youth in the community. Sarah was tragically taken from us when she was killed by a hit-and-run driver.

On August 5th, 1970, Sarah pulled twin girls, Amelia and Elizabeth Sommers, from the rushing waters of West River after they were swept off the bank by a tree that had been struck by lightning.

Presented by the Sommers family and Mayor Jake Kent on August 5th, 2010, the 40th Anniversary of the twins' rescue.

-╫-

Grace Keating was born in a Canadian east-coast university town, at the tail end of a large family of storytellers. When not working freelance in the world of theatre, television and film, and when not moving from east coast to west coast to east coast, she spends her time writing. She has enjoyed success with her short stories, having previously won the SLO Nightwriters award for *The Phone Call*, had three stories published in an anthology, and recently been short-listed by the Cambridge Short Story Prize for flash fiction with *Fish Tank* and *Upper Her, Lower Him*.

B.H.S.

By BethAnn Ferrero

The light reaches out but makes no contact. No one can see it now. Some might wonder if it exists at all—as a holographic ripple of chaos, maybe, or a radiant kaleidoscope of warped passageways. But far be it from me to divulge such things. That chance has passed. The sun has set on *that* horizon, one might say. It does sort of tickle my belly, though.

At least I have my sense of humor to keep me company as I sit here growing larger and larger—perpetually watching the horizon for my next meal. Some might consider me a ruthless warden of souls. An unrelenting slumlord, permitting none to escape my clutches. Imprisoning passersby in my own personal *Hotel California*.

Go ahead, try to leave. I dare you.

I'm not offended by that unsavory characterization. To be honest, I'm delighted by it. I thought I had it good before—back when my reputation was stellar and my ideals in sync with the universe. I mean, *everyone* knew my name. Learned men, philosophical dreamers, rock-and-roll bands, even pint-sized pubescents in overcrowded classrooms. Though it may be hard to believe, looking at me now, my future was bright and respectable. That is, until my heart gave out and my whole world collapsed.

But now, though others in my position might find it a lonely existence, I've never felt so alive. Or experienced such exhilaration. And the longer I'm here, the more I consume, the more magnificent I become: one stray morsel at a time, crossing right into my path. What can I say? Others are drawn to me—like iron to a magnet. And each bite makes me better, sculpting my physique and filling me with new and unbounded energy. Among the ranks of wrestlers, I am the sumo. On a plain of mole-hills, I stoop to peer down at the mighty Everest.

I do see a few others working the neighborhood from time to time. The smart ones, making their rounds. Clever enough—or should I say, *cowardly* enough—to stay just outside my reach for fear I might eat them.

And I would, too. Eat them. I can't help myself. I *must* catch up to Cygnus and Cygni. They're the real big shots around here. They're on the map! Unlike me. I haven't been discovered. Not yet, anyway. But give me time. I have a singular focus, unlike either of those two collections of dust and farts.

Oh, look there! On the horizon. A meal. Floating unwittingly toward me.

I draw it closer, effortlessly taking it within my grasp and swallowing. Extending my belly with its mass. Another satisfying feast.

Just wait. One day some pocket-protected, skyward-gazing astronomer will find me and everyone will know my name again. Cygnus and Cygni will have their turf, and I'll have mine. It's only a matter of time—and that's something I've got "light-years" of. Just ask any of my happy tenants.

I'm the most powerful force in the universe, and I'm here waiting, eagerly surveying the horizon. Drop by anytime. Visitors are always welcome—even if you can't see the light anymore. Holographic chaos and all that.

"Who am I?" you ask. I'm the Milky Way's fastest rising star— No, wait, I've already died. Let's try that again. I'm the Milky Way's yet-to-be-discovered fiercest and funniest member of the Black Hole Society. "B.H.S."—for those in the know.

＋＋

BethAnn Ferrero is a twenty-year Air Force veteran now completing the Creative Writing MFA program at Western State Colorado University. Her career has taken her around the globe and afforded her more fun than an engineer should have—from flying in jet planes to space acquisition. In part, her writing reflects the spirit, exhilaration, stress, and even the occasional implausibility and sorrow of those experiences. As for her serial-killing characters, their inspiration remains a mystery. Her dark fantasy short fiction "The Inheritance" can be found in the Shohola Press anthology, *Abandoned Places*.

The Pea and the Princess

BY Stephanie Vance

The phrase "like two peas in a pod" never applied to me. I was always one ginormous, rock-hard, unconquerable pea. Don't pity me, though. While those smug soft peas became pea soup, I sat in a place of honor on a shelf in the royal kitchen, heralded as the pea no one could cook. Chefs from all over the kingdom came at me with knives, cleavers, skewers, clubs, and boiling water, all trying to make me just another ingredient in a pea puree or side dish of peas and carrots. One enterprising genius even tried a blow torch. As part of the subsequent legal settlement, he received a tenured position as head chef, a nice little house in the country, and a firm commitment he'd never need to go near me again. So he has no reason to complain. Plus, I'm sure his eyebrows and mustache will grow back someday.

After that incident, the staff and I reached an understanding—a mutually assured destruction sort of thing. At first, I really liked not being attacked with kitchen implements. Everyone with incendiary devices stayed away from me, and the scullery maid dusted me three times a day. There's nothing so soothing as a nice feather dusting.

My satisfaction slowly turned to despair, though, as loneliness and a sense of underappreciation crept through my tough skin. Night after night, I watched the chef transform other lowly legumes into scrumptious meals adored by the royal family, things like pea-filled ravioli with white wine sauce and spring pea salad. As more and more compliments poured in from the King, I became more and more depressed. When would my turn come to be complimented? What did I bring to the table, as it were? Turns out everyone needs a purpose. Even peas.

In the midst of one of my lowest days, when the chef had just sent out a universally-praised pasta with green pea pesto sauce, the Queen came into the kitchens.

"There's another waif at the door claiming to be a princess," she grumbled. "That's the last time I let my son put out a general call for a beautiful princess of modest means. Turns out you can't throw a rock in this kingdom without hitting one."

"Too true, M'Lady. Too true," said the chef, nodding his head in what I'm sure was an attempt to look solemn. Unfortunately, without eyebrows it came off as surprised.

"After that Cinderella fiasco, I need to test this new waif before I introduce her to my son," she continued. "Put together a feast that forces her to use every piece of silverware we have—from the oyster fork to the grapefruit spoon." After much curtseying and bowing, the kitchen staff got to work. Then the Queen caught sight of me.

"What's this?" she asked, jabbing rudely. Peas have feelings too, you know.

"M'Lady, that's the hardest pea in the world. You know, the one that—" With shaking fingers, the chef smoothed his upper lip where his mustache used to sit.

"Hmm…I'll take it with me. A backup in case the silverware thing doesn't work," she said.

"M'Lady, I really wouldn't—" said the chef, moving to stand in front of her.

She cut him off with a withering "are you going to argue with your Queen?" look. It's a very specific expression only the most majestic of queens can pull off.

"You were saying?" she asked, her eyebrows raised.

The chef succumbed to the authority of the royal eyebrows and stepped aside. "Fine, Your Majesty. Have at it," he mumbled.

I practically jumped into the Queen's hand, and bounced in

excitement all the way up to the second level. Windows! Stairs! Carpets! Lights! Walls! Faced with so many new things, I barely noticed when she took me into a bedroom and shoved me under forty mattresses and feather beds.

"No real princess will be able to sleep with that thing under the mattress," the Queen muttered.

Wait, what? That thing? That *thing*? How dare she? I was as aghast as a pea can get. And like that, I knew my purpose in life. It was to help the waif or princess or vagabond or tramp or whatever this girl was get the upper hand on the pea-hating Queen. I just hoped the girl wasn't as empty-headed as most fake princesses.

After I stewed all day and into the night, figuratively, the door to the outer chamber finally opened.

"Here's your chamber, sweet Princess," said the Queen. "The bedroom is through the door at the end. If you have any problems—anything at all—do feel free to come to my audience chamber. Even at night, the guards there will be able to take a message to me."

"A thousand thanks, fair Queen. Goodnight." The Princess's voice wafted into the room and hung there like gossamer wings. Her dulcet tones told me she was, indeed, as sweet and unsuspecting as I'd expected. Ugh. Then the door clicked shut and the sweet voice turned grim.

"After that ridiculous display of cutlery, precious Queenie's got to have something in here she thinks will test me," she murmured. Sounds of searching filled the front room—cupboard doors opening and shutting, rugs moving, windows slamming. I was impressed. The girl had some serious searching skills. Desperate to get her attention, I screamed, thrashed, pushed, wiggled, moaned, cried, and squawked. Then I squirmed, writhed, howled, and shook. I even frenzied, to the extent that can be used as a verb.

Turns out a pea can't really do any of those things. I'd nearly given up hope when the wanna-be princess stepped into the bedroom and started gagging.

"What is that God-awful smell?"

Have you ever smelled a pea that's sat in a kitchen for years and then been smothered under forty mattresses and feather beds for over twelve hours? It smells like …well, in this case it smelled like success.

"Her Royal Snootiness is going with the pea in the bed routine? Amateur." The crushing weight on me lightened as mattress after mattress shifted, and the princess chortled when the last one came off. She lifted me and held me up to the light. I didn't glitter or anything because, you know, I'm a pea. But she must have liked what she saw.

"It's a bit unconventional, but I think you'd be a great center stone for an engagement ring, don't you agree?" She stuck me in her pocket and opened the chamber door. "Now, let's go tell my soon-to-be mother-in-law the good news."

Were I able to smile, I would have. As I bounced along in my princess's pocket, I realized, though she may not be all sweetness and light, we were going to get along just fine. I had fulfilled my purpose in life.

⊦⊦

Stephanie Vance lives in Washington, DC, where she works as a grassroots advocacy consultant helping people communicate more effectively with their elected officials. So that's a challenge. Her fiction work has appeared in the anthologies *Enter the Apocalypse* and *One Star Reviews of the Afterlife*, as well as the magazines *Bark Magazine* and *Andromeda Spaceways*. She's currently pursuing an MFA from Western State Colorado University.

Tuff

BY C. Flynt

We are older than old. Older than ancient. When Mother Earth was young, we were among Her firstborn.

As bright sparks of flame, we spewed from liquid fire and strove to touch the heavens. But we were made of clay, not fire, and as we cooled, we fell as ash to the ground. There we reunited with the liquid fire, spreading death as we moved. We burned trees, filled the rivers and poisoned the land. We fell from the sky in uncounted multitudes, layer after layer, shrouding the Earth.

Others followed, disgorged in their turn by new volcanoes, explosion after explosion, year after year, millennium after millennium. Each new layer pressed us together until pressure and heat formed from our multitude a single mass too heavy to move.

So we lay on Mother Earth's breast, immobile and unchanging. Above us shone stars older than even our Mother. Unlike us, they were mobile, circling the skies each night, though their paths never varied. With nothing to distinguish one span of time from another, we ceased measuring time at all.

But Mother Earth was not finished with us. Once more She thrust us toward the sky, sculpting us into rugged mountains. Freed from darkness, we overlooked the newly formed valley. We found the constant change of the landscape fascinating. The rivers ran clean, depositing silt and loam along their banks. This rich soil encouraged growth. The grasses grew first, then shrub, then trees. Then the animals, the fish, and the birds discovered this abundance and stayed. They lived their short lives, died, and returned to the soil. Mother Earth allowed no waste. She recycled old into new, each generation nourishing the next—small changes in a constant cycle.

We stood silent watch, rooted in the infinity of time. Perhaps we slept, lulled by the slow, steady beat of our Mother's heart.

The coming of humankind woke us.

Bustling, restless creatures whose lives lasted mere decades, they were the weakest of the animals, yet they ruled the valley. They were slow, but could run for miles and wear down their prey. They lacked natural protection, but fashioned coverings from hide and fur. Their complex brains gave them cunning, and their hands—those unique, grasping hands—gave them dexterity. They did not adapt to their environment. Rather, they reshaped it to their liking.

They were builders. They built tools and weapons, and huts for shelter. They shared their knowledge and worked together in groups. They built communities, joining their strengths to reduce their weaknesses. As we had, they joined to form a stronger whole. Entertained, we stood both witness and audience to their hustle and bustle.

Then the humans turned their tools on us, dragging us onto their stage. They drilled holes in our rock faces, then pounded wooden wedges into the holes. They drenched the wedges with water from the river, until the wood swelled deeper into our crevices, splitting us apart. We, who had so long been one, were once more broken into smaller groupings. The humans plied their tools, reshaping us into large blocks, which they laid atop one another to form a structure larger than ten of their homes put together. Some of our blocks were square, and others shaped into triangles and laid against one another to shape arches. Once again, pressure kept us together. But this was a lesser pressure. We were weaker as blocks than we had been as a mountain. We faced the mountain from which we were taken, and mourned our loss.

Time, once immeasurable, became our enemy. Winds, rains, and snows beat at us, carving lines one ash layer at a time. The humans performed their rituals to their god, scarring us with smoke and incense. Their young defaced our walls. Each year, we were less.

Then new humans came, bringing new gods. The competing followers slew one another in bloody carnage. The victors pulled down our walls, broke us into different blocks, then built us back into a temple of their own design. We who had slept though eons encountered change in the space of decades.

We learned a new time marker: generations. The humans morphed in generations. And we morphed with them. Before we could acclimate to one form, we would be reshaped and rebuilt into a different one. Our only constants were the stars and the mountain from which we had come. We found comfort in their stasis.

And then a star disappeared.

We witnessed a sharp flash of light and then saw nothing but the dark curtain of the night sky. Mother Earth joined us in our dismay. We rolled with Her as She trembled, and even the facing mountains slid deeper into the ground, as if diminished by the loss.

How could this be? How could the constants—the mountains, the stars, the Earth—vary? It was not in their nature, our nature, to shift so.

The humans took little notice of these events. They watched the star and repaired the small fissures in their buildings. Change was their sole constant. They were comfortable with it, and even sought it out. With such an ephemeral existence, they risked little.

Had they infected us when they broke us apart? Had the shaping and reshaping of their structures doomed us to their fate?

For millennia, we had watched the cycles of the different species in the valley. That which came from Mother Earth returned to Her; we had seen this over and over during our interminable lifetime. And we, too, came from Mother Earth. Would we, too, return to Her?

Our stones eroded over time, and we became the dust beating against the face of our mountain. Each time we touched the rock, we clung tight, defying the wind to return to the strength of our former union.

Even so, it was not as it had been. We had experienced transformation. We had faced mortality. Our siblings that had remained with the mountain denied the truth we shared with them. But sometimes, when the winds blew gusts to flatten everything standing in the valley, our restive mountain trembled.

Last night, a new star was born in the sky near where we watched the old star disappear. Was this another cycle? Would we be reborn when at last we returned to Mother Earth? Would She, too, wear down to death followed by rebirth?

And does that repeating cycle—birth to death to rebirth—grant us a kind of immortality?

We shall ponder this over the next eons.

-++-

C. Flynt is the husband-and-wife writing team of Clif and Carol Flynt. Clif is a computer programmer and technical book author (*Tcl/Tk: A Developer's Guide, Linux Shell Scripting Cookbook*). Carol has followed multiple careers, finally retiring as a freelance bookkeeper. Both are musicians and singer-songwriters. They live in a house they designed and built in the middle of a forest. They amuse the three cats who own them with hours of argument over plots, themes, characters, grammar and whose turn it is to write the first draft. To their happy surprise, these intense—ahem—conversations strengthen their stories and their marriage. They write science fiction, historical fiction, fantasy, romantic suspense, and query letters.

The Playful Protector

By Jasre' Ellis

You love Them, you truly do. It's just so cute when you tease Them a bit, and They make it so easy!

Maybe you should introduce yourself. You're a scarf, but not just any scarf. You're a long, luxurious silk scarf, hand-crafted from only the finest of silks, woven from the royal silk-worms personally kept by the Princess of—

None of that is true. Sorry.

You're a polyester-blend satin scarf. You were bought at a rather well-known beauty supply chain store, though! And you happen to have the most important job in the world: you keep hair safe.

This is not just any hair. You keep the hair of a kind, gentle, sweet and loving person safe. Them! And you take this job very seriously. Their hair is a gorgeous umber brown, nearly black, an even richer color than the lovely deep tone of Their skin. They have tightly-coiled curls that can spring back into shape when pulled, that can be stretched from Their ears to the middle of Their back, and can be braided and knotted into such intricate styles it would leave you in awe. They refer to it with odd alphanumeric codes—3b, 4c, etc. All you know is that Their hair is wonderful, curly, and yours to protect.

As Their satin scarf, it is your sworn duty to protect Their curls from getting frizzy and from breakage due to the malicious abrasiveness of Their cotton pillowcase. They take time each night to painstakingly wrap and knot you around Their hair, carefully tucking in sections, like folding an ornate dinner napkin. Their hair is a treasure, and you are honored to guard it.

But sometimes you can't help but be a bit playful. If They're not careful and tie a knot that's slightly too loose, you can't resist catching on a rough spot on the pillowcase to let the knot untie itself. You'll slip off and They'll wake up a little frizzier than They wanted, but They'll only have to add some product to fix it!

In one of your prouder moments, you flew all the way across the room, to be found on the floor there come morning. It was a hot summer night, and They had several small fans blowing throughout the room. You worked yourself loose and slipped across the sheets. To your utmost delight, one of your corners caught the stream of air from a fan and it whisked you from the bed. Instead of falling to the ground, you fluttered through the air, carried by the fans to the opposite side of the room. The look of absolute bewilderment on Their face was priceless!

While you do enjoy having fun, you must ensure you're never deemed expendable. You've seen many others come and go, not just from Their room but in the entire house. Some scarves met unfortunate ends, as cat bedding or a new collar for the dog. Once, a scarf dared get caught in the washing machine. It wound up ripped in half, and then there were two of them! They managed to be refashioned into hair bows, so you figure things could have been worse.

You'd rather make sure you keep your place. You're grateful They use you; Their sister replaced *all* of her scarves with a bonnet. *It* thinks it's so much better, so much more mature because of its fancy elastic band. You'll never be replaced with one of those things. They had to borrow Their sister's once when They lost you underneath a pile of clothes, but the band irritated Their skin and They gave it right back! So you're definitely confident you have a permanent spot by Their side—

Wait.

What's that?

Their mother comes in and walks over to the bed. She strips off the cotton pillowcase to replace it with something bearing a familiar sheen.

A rival. Panic.

Has your time finally come? Are you being replaced? Is this the end?

You're normally kept in a cubbyhole near Their bed labeled "necessities" with the other hair products They use daily. A ray of sunlight peeks through the curtain and glints off the new pillowcase. You direct every feeling of ire in your thin body towards it. How dare it come in and try to usurp your rightful place? No bonnet or pillowcase will ever love Them like you will! As you sit tucked into your usual spot, a nervous shiver runs through you.

Well, maybe you have been teasing Them too much lately . . . But it was all just in fun! Though, if you're being completely honest with yourself, it was mostly your fun at Their expense. They were never really in on the joke and always came out of each exchange a little on the frustrated side.

Hm.

Maybe you've had this coming.

Fear grips your satin. This could truly be the end. What use is a satin scarf that doesn't want to stay on its owner's head? Its only purpose is to protect hair like Theirs from the moisture-sapping, frizz-inducing outside forces. How can you possibly compete against something like yourself except . . . better?

You spend the rest of the day lost in thought, now ignoring the sheen of your replacement. If today is your last day with Them, you shall take comfort in being surrounded by Their other beloved products, knowing that you were well used and well loved.

They come back home late in the afternoon. You can hear Them chatting and laughing with Their family downstairs. You wait in terrible anticipation, knowing your days of being by Their side are numbered. Finally, They come into the bedroom, yawning and fumbling around. They turn towards you and your breath, if you had any, would have caught in your throat.

Just like always, They reach out to you with a gentle touch. You flow through Their fingers as enticingly as possible begging for Them to see how lovely you are. That you're sorry for every game you've played, that they were just meant in fun. You silently plead with Them to see how lovely you are, to remember how you've grown to contour yourself to Their head over the years, to recognize how well you know Their hair and its needs. That pillowcase is nice, but it could never care for Them like you do.

In a surprising turn of events, They raise you to Their head, just like always, and wrap you around Their newly twisted hair with gentle security. They finish with two familiar knots at the start of Their hairline and at the base of Their skull. Elation wants to spread through you, but you're frozen by the combined weight of relief and shock.

They're keeping you?

They're keeping you!

You're so caught up in your excitement that you forget about touching the pillow! When They get in bed and lay down, resting Their head and you against the pillow case, you feel another brief spark of panic. How is this going to work? Against cotton, you know how to maintain your grip around Them, ensuring not a single strand of Their coils drags against the surface underneath.

But against more satin? Won't you be too slippery? This must be a test. When They realize you can't hold up against the unyielding wall of the satin pillowcase, They'll toss you like the others. You hope They'll put you with the cat. At least there you'll be cuddled and loved as opposed to being out running around with the dog.

As the night goes on, though, you notice how comfortable it is to sleep against another smooth surface. It even helps support you, making sure not to pull at you and expose a strand of Their precious curls. You don't have to keep your attention split between maintaining your grip on Them and keeping a rough surface away from Their hair.

Maybe They weren't trying to replace you. Maybe They discovered a new way to make you both more comfortable. The cotton was always awfully abrasive and would take advantage of any weak points in your knots. Sure, being a little mischievous seemed fun at the time, but maybe the—you cringe; you really don't want to admit this—maybe the bonnet was right. It's still a smug jerk, but there is definitely something to knowing you're capable of this kind of security.

As They shift in Their sleep and gently rub Their head against the pillow, you relax as the pillowcase gives you both a soothing embrace. Rather than the end, you muse, this could be the beginning of a great partnership. It could maybe even be the beginning of a great friendship. You can almost feel the hum of contentment from the pillowcase echoing your own.

Actually, wait. That was just Them starting to snore.

The pillowcase seems to bristle beneath you, and a familiar, impish feeling of mirth bubbles up. There are always other sources of amusement to be found . . .

-+-

Jasre' Ellis is a black, nonbinary young professional from North Carolina. Jasre' drifted through high school and wound up with the odd double bachelors combination of Psychology and Japanese. Jasre' is currently studying to become fluent in Japanese with the intent of becoming a translator, so wish them luck! Jasre' has a passion for coming up with ideas for stories they'd love to see published and has come to terms with the fact that they'll just have to write it themselves to see it brought to life. They use their love of Japanese pop culture and expensive hobbies as well as their personal experiences with race and gender as inspiration for their writing.

Twenty Sides to Every Tale

By Laura Johnson

It was every die's dream to be purchased, to be played with and loved, and to go on adventures. Kederisa had been sitting in the loose dice jar at Hobby World for months, waiting. She wasn't exactly sure why. She was of a popular enough shape—dice with twenty sides were often used in role-playing games like *Dungeons and Dragons*—and decently priced at a dollar. Her colours were pretty, in her opinion. She was one of those split-coloured ones you might stumble across in a one-pound bag of assorted dice: glossy black and silver with acid green numbers. Sometimes customers rummaged around in the jar. Once or twice a week, people even picked her up in consideration and rubbed her sides with their thumbs, but they didn't purchase her.

She hadn't given up hope. Occasionally, she tried to strike up conversation with the other dice in the jar, but they'd long since stopped talking to her. She'd tried shouting at customers, but her words fell on deaf ears. The owner of the store couldn't hear her pleas to be showcased more favourably, and he seemed unperturbed by the lack of interest in the dice jar. For all their chatter, humans just couldn't *listen*.

One January afternoon, a young man entered the store. *Oh, he's a cute one,* Kederisa thought, even as she shivered in the draft. Snowflakes dotted his hair, and through the mop of curls she could see the pink tips of his ears. He strode over to the display of miniatures—figurines of warriors, mages, goblins, and firedrakes—and crouched to inspect them. After a minute, he straightened. Kederisa couldn't see what he'd selected, but her curiosity was piqued. He must be a role-player; some of them purchased miniatures to represent their characters during games.

They also loved dice.

To ordinary people, a die was just another game piece, rolled in games of chance or board games, always with six sides. Nothing special. To role-players, dice were magic. Gods, how she wished she were. Then she could teleport out of the jar, levitate to make herself more appealing . . . but alas, she was just an ordinary die. Kederisa had seen dice with as few sides as three and as many as one hundred in her time. *But none of them ever end up stuck forever in the dice jar.*

She tracked the man's movements as he meandered around the rest of the store. It was agonizing to wait, to see what else he purchased, yet he seemed content to browse. Finally, he moved toward the cash register. He paused at the counter, then turned to the dice jar.

"O mighty gamer," she intoned, "surely, you also need a new die! Free me from this prison!"

As if he'd heard her, he dipped his hand into the jar. After a few moments, his fingers closed around her. "Huh," he said. "Haven't seen this one before. You'll do perfectly for my new rogue."

A rogue? A wizard would have been cool, but she'd also heard that rogues got into all sorts of mischief; she'd never be bored again.

And so, just like that, Kederisa had an owner.

Nobody warned her about the vindictiveness of some humans.

———

"There was a hallway full of statues," Carlos said. "Incredibly. Lifelike. Statues. It's not my fault you guys charged into the room with a Gorgon. We went over this last session."

Wednesday night was game night for Benjamin, Kederisa's new owner. Carlos was the Game Master, whose role fell somewhere between narrator, referee, and God. Kederisa liked him immediately for his freckles—which reminded her of dice pips—and bright blue eyes. To the chagrin of Benjamin, Nate, and Paula, their entire party had died, having been turned to stone after a brief fight with the snake-haired monster.

"It was my zarking *dice*," Benjamin said. "If I hadn't rolled so horribly, I'd have taken out the Gorgon, no problem. These dice are cursed." To emphasize his point, he tossed his current favourite, Aric, across the table. Kederisa couldn't see the outcome, but the rest of the group laughed, so she supposed he didn't roll "horribly" that time.

Upon returning to the dice bag, Aric was inconsolable. "It was an awful session," he said. "Benjamin threatened to microwave me—because of his own stupidity!"

"That's ridiculous," Kederisa said. "Nobody would *actually* microwave a die. He was probably just upset." Benjamin wouldn't do that, right? He was their owner. Still, she shuddered at the thought of being melted.

———

Her first session began uneventfully. The characters met each other in a tavern, answering a call for work from one of the Magisters at the Academy. After a scuffle with some goblins to bond them as a party, they set off to complete their first real mission: to retrieve a stolen artifact from a bandit camp. It was during this mission that Benjamin rolled Kederisa for the first time. Kederisa's mind was a maelstrom of excitement and nerves.

The group made their way to the heart of the bandits' den and soon had the leader at their mercy.

Benjamin's face was positively mischievous. "I tell him, 'You're going to show us where your hidden stash of treasure is, or we're going to kill you.'"

"Okay, roll Intimidation," said Carlos.

Benjamin picked up Kederisa and blew on her. Her mind raced with anticipation. "Don't let me down," he said.

A knife twisted in her heart. Carlos never spoke to his dice like that.

Oblivious, Benjamin rolled anyway. His eyes lit up. "First natural twenty of the night! How do you like them apples?"

Suddenly, Kederisa was his new favourite. Set apart from the rest of his dice, she was the one Benjamin trusted to make his attacks and skill checks. He would caress her and puff hot air on her before rolling, as if it could influence the result. But dice didn't always roll high; probability didn't work that way. There would come a time, she knew, when she would roll low.

"There's always a honeymoon period with him," warned Skisron, a pyramid-shaped die who often joked that he was a caltrop. "It won't last. Soon enough, you'll be forgotten like the rest of his D20s. Or worse."

It was the "or worse" that made Kederisa afraid.

———

"I've got quite the dungeon crawl for you today," said Carlos as he unfurled his square-grid battle map and procured a green wipe-erase marker. He smoothed the map out, carefully pressing on the corners to flatten it. The surface was immaculate, free of stains and smudges. Kederisa wished it were his fingers rubbing her sides, instead of Benjamin's. Clearly, Carlos cared for his possessions. "To recap from last session: the Academy wants you to investigate a cult that they believe is trying to summon an Old God to this plane. They need you to find out if these men are just delusional scholars or actually dangerous. You've agreed to check out their base in exchange for a hefty reward. Do you have anything you wish to do in town first?"

Kederisa was almost dancing, and the other dice murmured in excitement. Dungeon crawls meant combat, which meant many dice rolls. And Old Gods—how exciting! Carlos had been working up to this session, for sure. The party had been exploring all over the kingdom of Givander, investigating strange symbols and packs of mutated animals. Benjamin, who played a dashing rogue, was often in the midst of the excitement as the party's scout and backstabber.

"I've got everything I need right here," said Paula, who played a half-demon sorceress and, given how much coffee she drank, had caffeine instead of blood. She cackled and cracked her knuckles. "All set to blow something up. Don't forget your lockpicks this time, eh, Ben?"

"What kind of thief do you think I am?" he snapped. Kederisa winced at his tone.

Carlos cleared his throat and continued narrating. The party had marched for almost a week to reach their destination, the Lost Temple. It had been a surprisingly easy journey. Usually, their Game Master threw monsters or bandits at them at night, but each watch went smoothly. Kederisa was secretly hoping for combat; Benjamin loved fighting in the dark. Instead, Carlos described an eerie stillness, frost that lingered well into the afternoon even though it was summer, and a growing *presence* in the land. On the seventh day, the group woke to a fog the colour of pond scum.

Nate, the party's paladin, said, "I call upon the holy light of Baenor to banish the mist. Can I make out any more details?"

"Light radiates from your shield, illuminating the road ahead of you up to about fifty feet away. The rest is impenetrable."

"What about my Orb of Seeing?" he asked. "Does it show me anything else of our surroundings?"

"When you pull it out of its silk pouch, it's so cold that the outside frosts over. You can't see anything."

"Don't you think the Academy would have already tried magic to penetrate this temple?" Benjamin scoffed. "Why else do you think they sent a band of adventurers? Let's just move on already."

"What if I step away from the path and deeper into the woods to try?" asked Nate.

"Are you sure you want to do that?"

Everyone knew what Carlos meant when he asked *that* question.

Take the second chance, she thought. *Who knows what horrors lurk in the woods?*

"I change my mind," said Nate. "I head toward the path and say, 'Come, everyone. Let us banish this evil!'"

The dungeon crawl began in earnest once the party reached the entrance of the Lost Temple. Carlos had one of those lilting, musical voices, and Kederisa's imagination painted quite the picture from his words. Built into a cliffside, what had once been a magnificent structure was now blanketed in moss. Runes were carved into the stone pillars, and the marble beneath them gleamed. At the back of the entrance structure, set into a stone arch, was a wooden door—somehow preserved amid the ruin—that led deeper into the mountain.

"Are the runes magical?" asked Paula.

After she cast *Detect Magic,* Carlos said, "Yes, they are. It's warding magic, meant to keep creatures away from this place. Like a magical 'No Trespassing' sign. You also notice more of them deeper inside."

"I approach the door and check for traps," said Benjamin.

This seemed to be Benjamin's reaction to everything. "Get on with it," he'd mutter under his breath. It grated on her, sometimes. Kederisa liked to be rolled, but she also enjoyed hearing the story unfold at a natural pace.

Benjamin clenched her in his hot, sweaty hands. She felt like she was suffocating. He rolled her, and scowled. "Seven, total." More muttering.

He had been like this every time she rolled less than a ten. Couldn't he understand that luck was beyond her control? Luck was its own magic; she wasn't a wand he could wave at each obstacle to make it disappear. If he always wanted to roll high, he should have purchased one of those sleazy weighted dice!

"You don't find any traps," said Carlos.

"Someone else check!" Benjamin snapped.

"You can't just not go in," said Paula. "As far as you know, it's perfectly safe."

Squinting at Kederisa in distrust, Benjamin said, "Fine. I open the door."

"And nothing happens," Carlos grumbled. "What's everyone else doing?"

———

Benjamin was never wrong—at least, not in his own eyes. When he was scouting ahead, one of the sentries attacked him and sounded the alarm. "What do you mean, they noticed me?" he demanded. "Paula cast *Invisibility*. I'm in-vis-i-ble."

"Benjamin," said Carlos slowly and deliberately, "did it ever occur to you that the cultists might have cast *See Invisibility*? Or have set up a tripwire?"

"Oh."

Kederisa sighed. While Nate was nearly religious about the rule book, he wasn't aggressive. And Paula, though she asked questions too, was new to the game and always thanked Carlos when he provided clarification. Besides, Carlos was the Game Master: he could adjust the rules if he wanted to.

At some point in that session, she started hoping she'd roll badly, praying to the Old Gods to grant her this wish. Benjamin wasn't just cantankerous—he was toxic. No wonder the other dice had sighed in relief when she joined the crew. Exhausted by his unreasonable demands of gaming and physics, they were happy for someone else to be the scapegoat. Kederisa felt heavy as Benjamin rolled her back and forth in his hand. All she had wanted was an owner, someone who loved the game as much as she did.

"His character deserved to be turned to stone," Kederisa said to Aric and Skisron. "If I were the Game Master, I wouldn't put up with him. 'Rocks fall, you die, goodbye.'"

"Carlos is too forgiving," agreed Skisron.

"Benjamin's being an ass," said Aric.

Then came the boss. While not explicitly stated, it was pretty obvious. Carlos described a cavern with cultists in the middle of a summoning ceremony, and a tentacled aberration forming from the acid green smoke. Clearly a boss.

Normally, Kederisa would be excited at the prospect of an epic battle. Instead, she felt sick. Nothing she rolled would be good enough for Benjamin.

"What is it?" Paula asked. "Do I recognize it?"

After a successful Arcana roll, Carlos said, "You haven't seen this particular creature before, but it looks like a Netherspawn, which has a nasty hypnotic gaze at close range. You also guess that, based on its tentacles and ring of teeth, it prefers to grapple and devour its victims."

If Benjamin's precious rogue is going to die, Kederisa thought, *this is the time.*

Armed with that information, the party began their fight. Nate, with his paladin, called upon divine protection to shield him as he drew the cultists' attention away from the others. With a burst of sulphurous smoke, Paula's sorceress rained hellfire down on all their foes. Benjamin's rogue sneaked around the side and felled a cultist from the shadows. As the battle raged on, and the cultists died, the Netherspawn fed on the corpses. More tentacles emerged from its body. Then it turned to the group in earnest, having run out of easy prey.

Do something rash, Benjamin. You know you hate playing it safe.

"Ben, pull out your crossbow," said Nate. "Let me tank it."

"I do more damage with my daggers," said Benjamin. "Besides, I have an exceptionally high Dexterity score. There's no way it can nab me."

As it turned out, it didn't need to. Instead, it fixed its hypnotic gaze upon Benjamin's rogue. He resisted the first attempt, to Kederisa's disappointment, but the next round he was not so fortunate.

"Make another save," said Carlos.

Benjamin picked up Kederisa. "Don't you let me down again," he growled.

To Kederisa's pleasure, she rolled a one—a player's nightmare.

"Well," said Carlos, "you're paralyzed. The Netherspawn grabs you with its tentacles and swallows you." At Benjamin's reddening face, he added, "You're not dead—but your character can't breathe, and he'll take acid damage every round until he escapes."

For a moment, Benjamin froze. Then he set Kederisa aside. Was he going to melt her? He ripped a piece of notepaper from his journal and, scowling, scribbled on the paper in jagged blue pen. She couldn't read it from her angle. He thrust her on the paper, forcibly turning her so her "1" was on top.

Kederisa wanted to cry. *This was humiliating!*

Nate peered over Benjamin's shoulder. "What's that? 'In a boss fight, I failed a save against paralysis and my owner got eaten by a tentacle monster'?" He laughed. "I've heard about dice shaming, but never actually seen anyone do it. It's okay, we'll save you."

"Quit being an ass, Ben," Carlos said. "Hell, you're holding up the fight."

"You're not the one whose character is being eaten! This die is cursed!"

Benjamin aimed his phone at her, blinding her in a flash of light. Then he dropped her into his dice bag. Everything went dark. At least she could still hear, imprisoned as she was: Carlos' voice, the rolling of other dice, and pencil scratches on character sheets.

Carlos sighed. "She's not cursed. Let me roll with her for a while."

"*Her?*"

"What's wrong with giving them a bit of personality? Here, borrow one of mine, the one you keep claiming 'never rolls below a fifteen'? Maybe it's not the die that's cursed. Maybe it's you."

Suddenly, the bag opened and light shone down from above. She fought back fear and repulsion as Benjamin's sweaty hand reached in and grabbed her. What would he do to her now? But with a flip, he just tossed her at Carlos, who caught her in his deft grip. His skin, like his smile, was warm. He gently set her down behind the screen that concealed his notes and dice rolls from the players, and a whole new assortment of dice greeted her with cheers. Then, the session continued.

Alas, a few rounds later, Benjamin's rogue triumphantly carved his way out of the Netherspawn's gut. The monster was still alive, but barely. After being healed by Nate's paladin, Benjamin went right back on the offensive.

It was with great satisfaction that she rolled a twenty for Carlos on the Netherspawn's turn. Kederisa snickered.

"That's a critical hit," said Carlos. The corner of his mouth twitched. He rolled some other dice for damage and calculated it. "The Netherspawn, irritated by the mortal stabbing him, slams his tentacles into you for fifty bludgeoning damage."

Benjamin stiffened. "This is ridiculous. My dice—"

"It's not your dice," said Carlos. "You're not invincible. You can't always stab things until they die. And bad rolls aren't the end of the world, you know. It's a role-playing game. They happen."

"These cursed dice!" Benjamin swept his hand across the table, scattering dice all over the carpet. "They want me to lose. And you can keep that one you're playing with—it hates me."

"Just watch," called Skisron from below. "I'm a magnet for bare feet."

Sure enough, Benjamin swore when he stood up. Every die in the room howled with laughter, as did the players.

"Yes, Ben, I'm sure they're conspiring against you," said Carlos with a twinkle in his gaze. He picked Kederisa up and squinted at her. "Wow, see how dangerous she is? Almost took out my eye."

Benjamin just scowled. "Don't mock me. Let's just get on with it."

Carlos resumed narrating, cradling Kederisa in his hand.

Finally, she thought, *I'm home.*

┼┼

Laura Johnson is a fantasy writer who resides in London, Ontario, where she is pursuing graduate studies in Psychology at Western University. When she's not writing for pleasure, she's immersed in academia, researching prosocial and antisocial personality traits. A huge geek, she enjoys playing *Dungeons & Dragons*, dressing up in cosplay at conventions, and gaming with friends. Previously, her stories have appeared in three anthologies by Bushmead Publishing—*Heroes*, *Monsters*, and *Scoundrels*.

Violet Sparkle

BY Kella Campbell

She knew she was beautiful from the moment they opened her packaging.

"Isn't this pretty?" she heard as the plastic came off. "Violet sparkle. They had some other colors too, but I liked this one, and I figured Brutus wouldn't care."

"Violet Sparkle? Sounds like a stripper name, not a color," a deeper voice said, with a laugh.

Violet Sparkle. That must be me, she thought.

"Let me see that." More laughter. "Puppy Pleaser Big Bone—textured silicone, and look at the shape of it! Did you get this for the dog or yourself, sweetheart?"

"It's a *dog* bone. For Brutus." This with a giggle. "You've got such a dirty mind. Where is he? Brutus, baby! Come!"

And that was when she saw him for the first time—all silky black-and-tan fur and hard muscle, lolloping toward her with alert interest in his big brown eyes.

"Who's a good boy? Sit for Mommy! Look what I've got for you . . . "

Brutus sat, panting, eyes fixed on her. The hand holding her reached down; the moment came. He took her in his warm, wet mouth, and it felt so good she wanted to vibrate with pleasure. But she couldn't move, had no options, no agency—all she could do was enjoy the chewing while it lasted.

For a while, it was wonderful.

Brutus carried her around, kept her in his bed. She got a bit slobbery, but that was okay, because she liked the way his breath smelled, and she knew the slobber meant she belonged to him. If she rolled under the stove or behind the garbage can, he yipped his help-me sound until a hand fished her out and returned her to him.

Oh, and the way he chewed her! He wasn't always gentle—there were a couple of tooth-marks in her pretty translucent silicone after a while, and she noticed a small bit missing from one end of herself—but it felt so good, and she knew she was still beautiful. Her bits of glitter still shimmered inside her. And Brutus loved her.

Then one day, the deeper voice called to Brutus, summoning him from a warm patch of sun where he lay curled up with Violet. "Brutus, buddy, I got you a new ball! Want to go to the park?"

Brutus bounded away without a backward look, and when he came home an endless time later, he had the ball in his mouth.

It was red, with a smooth curve and a fast bounce, and it smelled like synthetic bacon. *What's wrong with natural silicone?* Violet wondered, not being a scented product. *I smell clean when they wash me in the sink, or I smell like Brutus.* But he didn't seem to mind the red ball's fake bacon aroma.

He slept with the ball between his paws.

Later that week, Violet ended up under the stove, and no one looked for her.

Sometimes she heard the bounce-thud of the red ball, and the scrabble of Brutus's paws. Sometimes the giggle voice scolded, or the deeper voice laughed. She missed the kind hands that had washed her, the warm dog bed, the sunlight. But most of all, she missed Brutus.

Violet Sparkle wanted to rescue herself, but she couldn't even roll without a push to get started. She was only a dog toy, after all. She resigned herself to dust bunnies.

———

It wasn't entirely unusual for small things to make their way into the world under the stove—hair elastics, the safety seals from milk jugs, twist ties, the odd coin now and then, a plastic spoon, a chopstick.

A pinging noise and the skittering bounce of a small object were followed by a shriek and scrabbling hands. "My earring!"

The pretty little item rolled to a stop against Violet Sparkle. *It's beautiful,* she thought with pleasure, and remembered that she too was a sparkly and beautiful thing.

"It's okay, sweetheart, it's probably just under the stove. Let's get the broom." The deeper voice sounded reassuring. The earring would be rescued, no doubt, just as *she* used to get rescued when Brutus yipped for her.

Instead of a hand reaching in, though, the broom's straw bristles swept in, rushing all of them out into the light, every forgotten bit of nothing that had come to rest under the stove. And the pretty earring. And an utterly joyful purple dog toy who got to sparkle in the sun once again.

The earring was whisked up and away, and then Violet found herself being lifted too, as the deeper voice said with a laugh, "Hey, haven't seen this in a while. Brutus! Look! It's your stripper toy!"

She heard his paws before she saw him. Then he was there, jumping for her, grabbing her, running around the kitchen in a reunion lap of delight until the giggle voice told him to settle down. Pure glorious joy filled her.

That night she lay in Brutus's bed, cuddled between his paws. The red ball was gone—chewed to destruction, perhaps, or lost at the park? It didn't matter. Violet Sparkle was back where she belonged. Brutus hadn't forgotten her. She was loved.

Over time, there would be more and more tooth-marks, more bits missing, but the glitter embedded in her silicone would be there till the end; she'd always be beautiful to him, and to herself. No well-loved dog toy lasts forever, and she knew he'd eventually chew her to bits—but dog, what a way to go.

-++-

Kella Campbell can usually be found in Vancouver, Canada. She writes mostly romance, because love and relationships are what she finds most interesting about life and in fiction. Even when she dips into other genres, her writing almost always has romantic/emotional/relationship elements. Kella likes tea and dark chocolate and happily-ever-after endings. Visit kellacampbell.com to learn more.

Peter the Paper Clip

BY John Darling

Peter was getting very tired. After 10 years of holding together the paperwork for "Johnson, A.P.—SSN 555-66-33xx," his tensile strength was fading; he could feel his molecules beginning to sag. He was really getting bent out of shape. Lately, he found himself wishing that he could be relieved of this duty and maybe go on to do something better and more exciting.

As it was, he had not seen the light of day for a long time.

Before being shut up in this place, he remembered hearing his neighbor, who was holding a file together for "Jones, Samantha—SSN 639-22-45xx," say something about "long term storage." After the drawer they were put in banged shut for the last time, his neighbor became unclipped and Peter never heard from him again. No matter, he thought, 10 years ought to be long enough for anyone. It was unfortunate for him that he could do nothing about his predicament; unhappy as he was about everything, his only option was to wait and hope for something better.

———

When Peter heard a loud scraping sound of metal against metal, he knew something was up. At the same time he heard the noise, he also felt himself moving. He could see some light at the front of his row and he could see that some of the files held together by his co-workers were being removed. As Peter watched, he wished that the person doing the task would keep at it until they got to him. Even though the thought of change was a little frightening, it was also something he'd wanted for as long as he could remember.

Just as he was going to give up on this hope, his file was pulled out into the light. It was so bright that it reflected off the areas of his body that were not covered with rust. Before he could look around to see where he was, he was removed from his file and put into a clear container of some sort that held a bunch of his peers. Most of them, he discovered, had been holding files together in other areas. He even remembered a few of them from the original box in which they were delivered.

No one knew what was going to happen to them now, but they were all very happy to be out of their dark void, if only for a little while. Peter was overjoyed that he was close enough to the edge of the container so he could watch what was going on in the office. He had not seen anything for so long that even the seemingly routine work being performed fascinated him.

He saw the "Johnson, A.P.—SSN 555-66-33xx" file being taken apart, with some of its pieces being put into a blue pail with arrows on it and other pieces being put into a dangerous-looking machine that cut them up into smaller bits. He was sure glad no one had put him or his pals into that scary thing!

After a while, those who were doing the work went away and it grew dark again, but not as dark as the drawer he had lived in for the last decade. Now that all the activity had stopped, he was able to visit a little more with some of the other paper clips around him. In the darkness, they shared stories of what they had been doing before all these changes started. A few of them had been outside for all this time and some were new to the place, only being delivered in their boxes within the past few years. He also discovered that there were more varieties of himself than he ever knew about; some paper clips were bigger, some were smaller, some had sharp teeth (but were not scary), and some were coated with a soft, pliable material. It was so interesting to hear about their differences even though they were all somehow aware that the creation of each one of them had started in the same way.

No matter what their differences were, in shape, size, or how they came to be in this place, everyone felt rather certain that their futures would somehow be intertwined.

———

When the light came again, the work went on as it had the day before, and for the next few cycles of light and dark, nothing changed in the routine. Finally, though, during one light period, workers came in with wheeled things and removed the holding cases that many of paper clips had been in. If they could have jumped for joy, they would have, because now they knew for certain that they would never have to go back into that darkness.

A few more light and dark cycles passed with all the paper clips feeling great. Now and then, a sunbeam would find its way to their container and they would all bask in its warmth while remembering the heat that first formed them.

Finally, the workers started taking everything else out of the room the paper clips were in. Pictures and clocks from walls, desks, chairs and mats from the office area; Peter had begun to think that he and his friends would be left behind when at the last moment someone picked them all up and put them in a box, which was then moved out with the remaining items.

This started a wild ride for Peter and his pals.

Their small package was placed in another dark cavern that was almost as gloomy as the one they had emerged from a few days before. However, this place was much different. First, they all sensed that it was a larger space, and second, they all felt movement which made them feel great. What's more, none of them had to work; they were allowed to just lie in their clear container and sway with the motions of the cavern that held them.

Peter sensed that a few of the light and dark periods had come and gone since they were put into this place because it would stop moving for a while, then move again, and then stop once more in the light so things could be taken out of it. Peter and his pals again thought they were going to be left behind as the cavern emptied out, leaving them alone with a few other things that were made of steel like them.

It was during the next light period that Peter's life changed forever.

The door to the cavern slid open and rough hands pulled his box out into the daylight. His clear holding pen was removed and turned upside down so that Peter and his friends went into free fall. When they landed, they were in a round metal container with other things made of steel, but these things were bigger, heavier, and came in many shapes. They weren't anything like Peter and his pals.

Something came along and picked up their new home, and after a short trip, they were lifted up and dumped again, this time into a much larger container that was filled with some sort of liquid. Though it was harsh, it made Peter feel good as he soaked in it. After a time, the liquid was drained away and another milder liquid filled the vat he lay in. Soon that liquid also went away, and he and the rest of the steel objects were dumped into another container that was open to the sunlight.

Peter looked down on himself; he was beautiful. The rust that had been invading his body was all gone, apparently washed away with the liquids. His molecules felt stronger than they had in many years. He did not have much time to admire the change in his body before he and the rest of the metal objects were lifted up and dumped into the largest container yet. This one was able to move and soon they were all traveling again.

With all the switching of containers, Peter had lost track of most of his old paper clip friends, but as they went along, he came to know some of the others around him. One was a large oddly shaped piece of metal who said that he was a "fender" from an automobile, which was something used for getting from one place to another. It was like the thing they were in now but much smaller. One day his automobile hit another one and that was the last of both automobiles and both were taken away to be disassembled. Some of his other automobile sections were in the same container as he and Peter were, but most of his friends had been taken elsewhere, so Peter told him that they could be friends. The fender thought that would be nice.

All along the way, they talked about where they might be going and compared notes about where they had come from. It turned out that their beginnings were nearly identical. Both were born from iron ore. They had been extracted from Mother Earth, put into the heat, then formed and shaped. It was only how they ended up that made them different. Now they were together again, apparently headed for the same destiny, whatever it may be.

When the thing they were traveling in finally came to a stop, they were dumped again, this time onto some sort of metal strip that moved. During the transfer, Peter had become wedged into a dent in his new friend. This made him very happy. He felt safer with his new pal who'd been around so much in his time.

After a few minutes on the metal strip, they were in free fall again so Peter had to hang on to his friend for dear life. Though they crashed with a loud bang onto the bottom of their latest holder and more metal objects fell on top of them, Peter managed to stay put. For a long time, everyone just lay where they had landed; no one came to move them around anymore. Then some of the metal objects that were under them said that it getting very hot down there. Soon it became hot everywhere. He and his new friend began to lose their form, which frightened him until he realized that everyone else was melting too. It was the heat that had formed all of them coming to take them back again. Could it be that they were going to return to Mother Earth?

Peter woke up. He did not remember too much at first. The last thing he recalled was it getting very hot had which made him sleepy, and then he was here, wherever "here" was.

He heard a familiar voice call his name; the sound of it seemed to come at him from all around him. It was his friend, the fender. It seemed that they were still together but now even more so than before since they had been made into a part of each other. The fender told Peter that they had been melted and reformed into some enormous circular object. Hearing this, Peter looked around him for the first time. He could see outward for miles and miles. Apparently, he was part of a structure that towered high above Mother Earth. Looking left and looking right, he could see that the structure curved away in both directions. Looking up, he could see a great fin protruding out from one side. He asked his friend if he knew what they had become.

Having been out in the working world for years, the fender thought that they were part of some kind of flying vessel. He had seen fins, which were sometimes called wings, like these at times when he was driven to a place for airplanes. Airplanes could fly off the face of Mother Earth.

However, even the fender had never seen wings as big as these. Being larger than Peter, his molecules were spread out more, so much so that he could see the other side of their new object. He could see that they made up one of two large cylinders that were attached to a flying vessel.

Whatever this whole thing was, the fender thought that it was being made ready to fly.

Another voice spoke out, a former airplane part—he said he'd been an engine cowl, whatever that was, and he was famil-iar with the way they got flying machines ready for takeoff. From everything he was seeing, he told them, the fender was right. However, the machine of which they were now a part was much, much larger than the plane he had been attached to, so he thought it was going to be able fly higher and farther than he ever had, which made him happy but scared Peter a little bit.

Soon each object that had become one began talking almost all at once. Each one told what they knew about flying machines, even if they'd never been part of one before. Everyone was very excited. They talked for several light and dark cycles on end, with everyone reporting anything they saw on the ground far below.

Then, at the beginning of one of the light cycles, the huge machine began to shudder violently. Everyone fell silent in anticipation of what would happen next.

A searing heat began to build up inside of their circular object, and just as it seemed as if they were all going to be melted down again, they began to move, slowly at first, then as they got farther away from Mother Earth they took on great speed.

Though Peter was scared by this new adventure, the touch of his other friends kept him from crying out in fear. The larger, more traveled of them seemed to be in awe of what was happening, but none were frightened. So Peter looked down; he could see Mother Earth getting smaller with each passing second. Unexpectedly, they burst into a black void and the searing heat went away only to be replaced by shuddering cold. A loud explosion sent them into free fall again. Peter held on as hard as he could, knowing that a fall from this height would surely damage everyone, but after a few minutes it became clear that he did not need to hold on since neither he or his friends were falling.

Almost at once, everyone began to talk, speculating on where they were and why they could see all of Mother Earth but not go crashing into it. Then, from amidst the cacophony, a small voice spoke up, a voice that had been silent during all previous conversations.

She claimed to know where and what they were.

She had assumed what was going to happen before it did, but she did not want to say anything until she was sure of the facts, and now she was sure. She said that she had once been a tube that made up something called a telescope. This was a device used to look out into "outer space," the stuff that Mother Earth floated in. Through the lens of the telescope, she had seen other planets and the flying rocket ships that sometimes went to these planets. That was what they had been made into; part of a rocket ship taking a crew to another planet. Now they were floating, free from the pull of gravity. They must have been the holder for the fuel that got the ship off the planet—and now they had been discarded, most likely forever.

At first, this idea made everyone sad knowing that they were never to be used for anything ever again, after having been useful, large or small, from the day they were first mined out of solid rock.

So, for a while, everyone became quiet as they pondered their fate. Then his friend, the fender, spoke up. He said that though he too was unhappy about not being needed anymore, he planned to enjoy his retirement because you sure could not beat the view from up here.

As Peter's side of the cylinder turned slowly back to where he could see the small blue planet of his birth, he recognized the wisdom in his companion's words.

During his small life, Peter always wanted to be something more than that which he was created to be. Now, knowing that he was going to be up here for eternity while looking down on the planet of his birth, he was overjoyed with the knowledge that he would forever be surrounded by his newfound friends.

‑‑‑‑+‑‑‑‑

Since the 1970s, **John Darling** has written and published many short stories, poems, and magazine articles. His first publication was a short story which appeared in the *Journal of Mental Health*. His lone play, *Stage Directions*, has been produced in the United States, Canada, and most recently at the Soho Theatre in London, England. He has two books available. One book is a nonfiction account of how rock bands and performers chose their stage names; the other is a cookbook compiled from his grandmother's favorite recipes.

Cashmere

Z. Ahmad

I know it's a little vain, but I think I'm pretty. I've always thought so. Or at least, I have always thought I thought so. My earliest memory is of being dunked into a bucket of swirling watery green dye. I was dunked into the liquid repeatedly. With each dunk, I felt the cold emerald elixir against my skin, washing over me, coating me with a permanent dark green hue. The color was beautiful. Then I was laid out where warm sunlight could dance across my skin. They let me stay there until every trace of wetness had evaporated. Shortly thereafter, a woman tattooed my newly green skin. Her hands moved quickly, creating intricate designs with white thread. When she was finished, she ran her fingers all over me. I think she was looking for any defects in her work, but the tattoos were perfect. My tattoo artist then folded me up and placed me in a box with about 100 others like me. Although everyone in the box was gorgeous, I still think I had the best tattoos of the bunch. I began to feel an increasing sense of anticipation as the lid of the box closed. My pretty compatriots and I were going on an adventure! Or so I thought, but the journey was boring; everything was boring until I met my Esther. The day I met her, it was like all my hopes and dreams were realized. But I am getting ahead of myself.

There was a small hole in the box in which we were placed, which allowed me to mark the passage of time. At least 30 light-dark cycles happened before our box was once again opened. I remember the bright lights flooding us as the brown cardboard flaps were torn open. *Finally, my adventure,* I thought, as hands reached down into the box. The hands did not have the finesse of my tattoo artist's touch. The hands were rough. They did not appreciate my softness nor the intricate work of art that laid across my skin. With unwarranted brashness and speed, the rough hands tossed me to another pair of slightly softer hands.

"Hang these up by the green dress, they'll look good together."

"Okay, sure."

As the softer hands caught me, I felt so indignant. This was supposed to be *my* adventure, and thus far I had sat in a box and been roughly handled by two sets of hands.

Thus began the long process of waiting to be chosen. What a tedious process! I stared at the same rack of black blazers for weeks on end. Each time one of them would be selected for an adventure, the rough hands would replace it with another exactly like it. In the beginning, I would rejoice for a moment when people would notice me. But soon I noticed the trend. Some hands would pick me up, only to place me back down after looking at the tag that had been attached to my skin. Other hands would run their fingers over my skin, never picking up the hanger which I was on. But, they always looked at the tag. I hated that tag. It wasn't me. It wasn't my story. My story was in the adventure I was yearning to have, the beauty and skill of the hands behind my tattoos. That irksome tag felt like a noose holding me back from the world. This went on for some time, until I thought that it would be all of my existence. Then my Esther happened.

It started out like normal; I felt my hanger being picked up. Then old wrinkled hands felt my skin. I was ready for those hands to look at the tag and put me back down. Instead she called out, "This is beautiful, Esther, let me buy it for you. You've been saying you want a green one." Then I felt the gaze of my Esther's eyes for the first time. Her eyes seemed to be inspecting me.

"It is beautiful, but how does it feel?" my Esther said in a sing-song Southern accent as she stretched out her hands to take me.

She gently ran her fingers up and down my white tattoos. My

Esther then pressed my skin to her silky cheek. The heat from her cheek warmed me.

"It's so soft!"

She looked at the tag and smiled. This was the first time someone had smiled after looking at my tag. Her smile was the catalyst. It was as if all that resentment I had allowed to build up toward my tag disappeared. The noose that once held me back from the world had turned into a tether allowing me to safely explore the depth of world's wonder with my Esther.

"It's handmade by women artisans, and you are right, it is gorgeous, it feels great; it's a perfect scarf."

———

When I arrived at my Esther's home, I was surprised by how few creations like me there were. There was only one other in her closet! It did not have tattoos like me—rather, its skin was solid purple, much thinner than mine, with tassels at the ends. My Esther would take the purple one out and wear it often. I won't lie; I was a little bit jealous. What adventures they must've gotten up to! She had said I was gorgeous in the place with all the bright lights, but she never picked me. Day after day, I sat in that dark closet, lonely and bored. I would hear snippets of conversation here and there. Some of them were mundane, others hinted at the adventures I was yearning for, and then there were those I couldn't decipher.

"Y'all need to pick up some milk; we're out."

"Come to the pool with us."

"This summer is killing me—a hundred and ten degrees today."

"When are you going to Hawaii?"

"I'm detecting energies up to 10 GeV."

"Basically, it's an electron, only 200 times heavier."

My Esther liked talking about something called a muon. I had never seen or heard of these muon things before. The way her voice would speed up in excitement when speaking about detecting them, I knew she must love them. I thought her curiosity about them demonstrated her adventurer's heart. We had to be kindred spirits. But she didn't want me. Surely that smile had to have meant something. That smile couldn't just abandon me to a boring life—an adventurer would never do that to a fellow adventurer.

I didn't know it back then, but my Esther was waiting for something called "fall" to come, before she could choose me for an adventure. It was dark outside; that much I could tell. This was usually the time that my Esther would ready herself for sleeping, but tonight she seemed to be getting dressed in adventure clothing. As my Esther pulled me off the hanger, I thought to myself—finally, an adventure! Once I was off the hanger, my Esther wrapped me around her neck and pulled her scratchy hair off her neck and into a ponytail. My Esther did a quick once-over in the mirror before whispering the word "perfect" to herself. I smiled; I couldn't agree more—I looked perfect.

"Your ride is here, Esther."

"Okay, thanks for letting me know."

"What time will you be back?"

"Around dawn."

"Be safe."

My Esther ran down the stairs to meet her ride. Her heartbeat picked up as she opened the door and a swoosh of cold air hit me. My Esther, however, did not shiver; I was keeping her warm. She walked over to a darkly-colored pick-up truck and slid into the passenger seat.

"Nice scarf!"

"Thanks, it's new. So, where are we off to this time?"

"Enchanted Rock. We should be able to see the meteor shower from there tonight."

"I can't wait; I brought hot chocolate!"

"You didn't have to, but thanks."

"I know, but it'll be cold, and hot chocolate is good for the soul. Will we be far enough from Austin?"

"The light pollution shouldn't be too bad."

That night was magical. They say beauty knows beauty; when I saw the stars for the first time, I knew I had seen something more beautiful than myself. They were sort of like the hole in the box that took me from my tattoo artist to the rough hands that delivered me to my Esther, except that instead of being a single point of unwavering light like the hole in the box, the stars filled up the sky. There were twinkling points of light in every direction. I thought the brightening and dimming had to be telling some sort of grand story that I just couldn't decipher. There was even a milky silver haze that covered a portion of the sky. Oh, and the shooting stars! I think we saw at least fifteen. They would dance across the sky with short trails of glowing sparks. They looked so graceful, yet they had such power—not allowing any other star to stand in their path. My Esther began pointing out different star patterns in the sky to her friend.

"I always love finding Orion in the sky."

"Where is it?"

"Right there; that's his belt," my Esther said, pointing at a row of three stars.

She continued to name the stars until the sun came up. Once home, she placed me back on the hanger. I'd had my first adventure! Thankfully, it would not be my last one. We would go on to have many more stargazing and non-stargazing adventures together, until the day my Esther decided to send me on a new journey without her.

———

My Esther had transformed over the years. Her once spry and agile movements became slow and deliberate. But her character hadn't changed; she was still generous. Which is why a simple gift exchange caused me to be sent away from my Esther and to my next person, my Huma.

"It's just like the one you wear all the time so I knew you would love it," a small boy said as he beamed at my Esther.

"I adore it, Jamie," she said, hugging the boy and the thing that could be my twin except it had golden tattoos on its green skin.

The boy's sticky fingers pulled on me. "Put it on, Mrs. Esther."

My Esther obliged him, removing me from her neck and placing the new me where I'd been. The jealousy that had long since been extinguished by many adventures with my Esther slowly crept back into my thoughts. I wasn't as soft as I once was. My color had faded; my once-white tattoos had taken on a slight greenish tint. However, the design itself was still impeccable. Not a single loose thread. They were *much* better than those golden tattoos.

"Now that the presents are done, let's bring out the cake!" my Esther said as she walked into the kitchen, leaving the party behind. I was picked up by one of her friends.

"I'll help you," the friend said, following my Esther into the kitchen.

"I know you don't like having more than a few scarves, Esther . . . if you want, you can always return this one."

"No, it'll break his little heart. He'll think I don't like his gift. I can't." My Esther took me from her friend. "I'll just send this one to Goodwill; I really don't need two green ones."

=====

The journey to my Huma's was as uneventful as my journey to my Esther's. I was put into a dark box once again, and once again I spent several days inside. This box had several tiny holes, similar to the one in my first box. Unlike then, this time I had memories of the stars to pass the hours and days. In addition to using the holes to mark the time, I pretended they were the stars that my

Esther had shown me. At least twenty light-dark cycles repeated before the familiar bright lights came flooding in again as the flaps of the brown cardboard box were torn open. I felt foreign hands reach in to grab me. Before I could really gauge the hands, I was tossed into a pile of clothing, and was soon buried as other items joined me. I remained that way for what seemed like a long time. I was unable to keep track; it was just darkness. I thought it would never end. I tried to hold onto my memories, my adventures. The darkness made it difficult to remember my Esther. There were so many good memories, but my heart ached. I missed her so much. Then all at once there was a bright light and I was back on a hanger, on a rack not unlike the one my Esther had first rescued me from. This place was more crowded, though, and there was no one like me, just skin and tattoos. *Their* skin was fashioned into dresses, shirts, and other clothing. I couldn't see much. I was smushed between a pair of jeans and a sweater. Neither one was particularly soft. Soon, the old pattern of being seen but never chosen reasserted itself. My hanger would be pushed across the rack or picked up for a moment only to be put back down. No one looked at my tag, though. It was irrelevant to them. Hands would feel me, but never choose me. But anything was better than the darkness. I found peace once again in my memories. I was determined to be satisfied with never going on a new adventure. Then my Huma happened.

It started out in the usual way; I felt my hanger being picked up. Then warm hands felt my skin. I was ready for those hands to put me back down. Instead, a voice called out, "This is beautiful, Huma, you should let me get it for you. You've been saying you want a green one." I felt the gaze of my Huma's eyes for the first time. Her eyes seemed to be inspecting me just like Esther's eyes had before. I felt my anticipation growing. I would get to go on new adventures, after all.

"It is beautiful; how does it feel?" my Huma asked, as she stretched out her hands to take me.

She too ran her fingers up and down my now off-white tattoos. Then she looked at the tag and smiled. This was the first time someone had even looked at my tag since I found myself in this new crowded place. But even more exciting, her smile was a catalyst, just like my Esther's smile. It was as if all that hidden resentment I had allowed to build up towards my Esther for giving me up melted away, allowing me once again to explore a new world—this time with my Huma.

"It's cashmere from Kashmir! And you are right, it's gorgeous, and it is a perfect hijab."

=====

Her closet was beautiful. The last time I had seen so many like me was at my creation. Every color was represented. Some were rectangular, others triangular, while yet others seemed to be a strange circular shape with a cutout in the center. They were very orderly. Their placement seemed to create a rainbow in her closet. With this many like me, I was sure I would never get to go on any adventures, but anything was better than the complete darkness of the clothing pile. But I was wrong! Huma took me on an adventure almost right away. The day after bringing me home, she took me off my hanger. She placed me on her head, my green skin covering my Huma's dark curls. She spent several minutes staring at the mirror while she tucked her hair beneath the protection of my skin. Finally, she smiled at herself in the mirror and whispered the word "perfect" to herself. Although I felt a little strange being on top of her head instead of around her neck as I thought scarves were supposed to be, I could not agree more—I looked perfect.

"I'm off to the Planetarium."

"Okay, don't forget to get your volunteer sheet signed this time."

"I won't, and I'll text when I get there."

"When will you be back home?"

"Before dark."

"Okay, be safe."

My Huma locked the apartment door behind her and proceeded to take me on a new adventure.

"Nice hijab, Huma."

What was this hijab I kept hearing about? I was a scarf; that's what my Esther called me. Looking back on it now, I am ashamed of my silent hopes. I wanted nothing more than for a strong breeze to pull me down to my Huma's neck. Although I thought I was pretty wherever I sat, I believed that around the neck was where I belonged.

"Thanks, it's new. What topic did we decide on for the next show?"

I loved shows. My Esther had taken me to a musical several times. Some of them were great, while others were only slightly better than being in the pile of darkness. The curiosity was killing me. I had to know if I was going to be bored to tears.

"We're doing a comparison between the names different civilizations gave the same constellations and the myths that go with them. You up for the research?"

"You know me, I'm always up for the research." my Huma said, smiling.

"Yeah, you're a research fiend."

My Huma spent the rest of the day reading and highlighting. She highlighted paragraph after paragraph. Some stories I knew, like the myth of Orion. Others I had never heard of before like the Chinook Tribe story of the Two Canoes, or the Arab story of Al-Jabbar (The Giant) or the Hindu story of the Mriga (The Deer). They all referred to the same stars in the night sky. As I read along with my Huma I began to realize that sometimes the same thing is called by different names, and is used by the people to tell different stories, but in the end, they are talking about the same objects. Thoughts about fashion, religion, culture, scarfs, and hijabs swirled around me like the green dye that gave me my color, imbuing each thread of my existence with new knowledge. In a moment of clarity, I finally saw myself as both a scarf and a hijab. I didn't need to be around her neck anymore to feel fulfilled; her placement of me around her head was perfect.

While her research would take many days, and although I did not get to see every book my Huma would read, I knew the show would be amazing, even if I did not get to see it. As luck would have it, though, I did get to see the final show.

———

"Baba, I'm leaving for Friday prayers," Huma yelled over to her father as she wrapped me around her head.

"Okay, I will be going to the second Jummah prayers. What time is your show tonight?" he asked her.

"It's late, like around 9:00," she said as she walked over to the door.

"Ahh, so after Isha prayers. Will you be coming home then after Jummah?"

"No, I want to take a short walk in the park before heading to the planetarium; the weather is supposed to finally be nice."

"Okay, be safe."

"I will," Huma replied as she shut the door behind her.

———

The walk in the park is nice. The weather is warm with a soft breeze. A small gust causes me to slip backward on my Huma's head. Her hands effortlessly reach for me and tug me back up to where she prefers me to lie. Then all of a sudden, I hear an angry shout.

"You know, you're such a pretty girl. But you'd look much prettier without that thing on your head."

Who do you think you are? I look pretty no matter where I am. I am livid. My thoughts are swirling around me in an angry haze. I looked pretty in that old box with the make-believe stars. Though no one could see me, I looked pretty in that awful pile of darkness. I also looked pretty as countless people walked by me on the hanger, in both those places of brightness. I looked pretty as a scarf on my Esther's neck. And I look damn pretty as a hijab on my Huma's head. Where I am does not limit me. The next thoughts that cross my mind: Is my Huma okay? My Huma needs to be okay. My Huma's breath quickens as her heart beat accelerates. She opens her mouth to tell the ignorant fool off. I know she'll say something sassy and confident; that is just who she is, but I am still worried for her. The thoughts begin to swirl again. What if this escalates? What if this person has a bone to pick with my Huma? Why does this always happen when all we want is a quiet walk in the park?

"Leave her alone; she looks fine just the way she is," a woman says, as she uses her cane to propel herself up from her park bench.

The bully looks around and notices that other people are staring. With a shake of the head, the bully gives both the old lady and my Huma one last dirty look before scurrying off. My Huma turns around to look at the woman, who is slowly walking towards us. My Huma doesn't know the old woman, but the woman's voice has a familiar sing-song drawl to it, reminding me of my past. Her thick Southern accent causes me to recall my Esther's voice; how ridiculous, that was a lifetime ago. My Huma motions for the woman to stop walking. She can tell that every step is difficult for the woman.

"Thank you, but you didn't have to," Huma says as she hurries over to the woman. I can tell she does not want the woman to have to take even one extra step.

"You're welcome; I know I didn't have to, but I can't stand rude people. My ma taught me better."

"Me neither. What brings you to the city?" my Huma asks as she smiles.

"I'm here to see a show at the Hayden; I have always loved stargazing."

"Oh, me too! I actually volunteer there."

"Good for you; it's important to be involved in your community. Gift your community with your time, that's what my mother always said . . . she would have been 100 today, but she's been gone for a while now. She lived a long life full of love and family—" the old woman said, clearly lost in her own memories.

My Huma was used to this; she worked with all sorts of people, including the elderly. I feel my skin shift as my Huma smiles at the old woman. My Huma sits down on the bench next to the woman. "My name is Huma. Do you want to tell me about your mom? I am sure she was a great person to have taught you so much."

The old woman smiles, happy to have a companion to tell her thoughts to. "You know, the first thing you ought to know about my mom is that she was always generous. She loved gifting things; she actually bought me a green scarf just like yours once."

"She sounds like my mom," Huma says, laughing. "She bought me this hijab."

The old woman returns my Huma's mirth. "Mothers are the best—Oh, where are my manners? My name is Esther . . . "

I don't hear anything else. Did she say Esther? This is my Esther! I never thought I would see her again. What luck! My Esther, how I've missed you! I have been on many adventures since we've parted. I have learned much more about the stars from my Huma. Did you know that the Orion constellation has many other names? Do you remember the first time you showed me Orion, at that meteor shower? That was my first real adventure. Our stargazing trips were so exciting! Thank you for them. They got me through a lot of sad days. Thanks for standing up for my Huma. She could have done it herself, but it's nice not to have to. My Huma takes me on adventures too. We have to get out of the city, but when we do, we can really see the stars. And there are all sorts of adventures you can get up to in the city. They have lions here. *Lions!* Her family is nice, you would like them. They are always telling stories to each other, about far off places, and how things were when they were young. I think I like her grandmother's stories the best. She tells them in multiple languages. So, I get to learn a new language! Some of the words remind me of my tattoo artist's language. Oh—you know, come to think of it, I never really told you my story, the story of my tattoo artist and where I came from. We must remedy this immediately. My first thought as I came into this world was: it may be vain, but I am pretty . . .

-++-

Z. Ahmad describes herself as a Muslim American feminist physicist. She obtained her undergrad degree in physics from Southeast Missouri State University in 2011. She currently lives and works in Ohio as a research analyst. Although she has been writing and telling stories since at least the first grade, this is the first publication of her non-technical work. Ms. Ahmad draws inspiration for many of her stories from her experiences growing up in rural America as a daughter in a biracial family. In her writing, she enjoys exploring themes related to female empowerment, cultural intersectionality, science, and science fiction.

What I See

By E.D.E. Bell

The Comic Con is my favorite event.

When I was first installed, I didn't know what went on in the world outside the door. After all, the solid gray door stays shut except when the rod and flag prop it open. Even then, I can only see a few round tables. They seem nice enough.

My first memory was of a woman with a drill attaching me into place. She peeled off a piece of paper, and there she was. She was beautiful and she sang while she worked; a patch on her jacket said Sheila. I wish Sheila would have stayed longer, but I never saw her again. I wonder if there are other mirrors out there, in other rooms, for Sheila to bring into the world.

It seems unlikely that this is the only place with mirrors.

Sheila installed me on a wall, with two other mirrors, one to each side. Each of us was partnered with our very own sink—mine is the best, I think—and two hand dryers joined us on the opposite wall. The fancy kind that makes the people's skin wiggle! It's so funny when they do that.

I know there are toilets too, since I can hear them flush, but they stay in their own private rooms. Isn't that fancy! I'd like to meet them someday, though I'm not sure that would be possible.

The building is sometimes quiet and sometimes busy. That's nice, of course. When it's quiet, I can rest. Sometimes I don't think at all. But when it's busy, I take in everything I can. I meet everyone and remember their faces. I can remember them all.

I soon learned there are different events here. From what I can tell, events are like huge parties where people of all different types come together and smile and it looks like they buy things also. How wonderful for those items to be purchased! I wonder if I was purchased too.

There are holiday shows and equipment shows and garden shows, and those are all fine. But my favorite happens just once every year—it's called the Comic Con.

I'm not exactly sure why they call it a con; it seems perfectly honest to me. But I've learned what comics are: beautiful images that tell a story in all the colors of the world. And the people who attend dress up just like the characters in their pictures. They bring them to life! Lots of people visit me, whether to get ready, or check their face, or just to wash their hands.

A few do not wash their hands.

At the Comic Con, people stare at themselves a lot. And it's my job to help them.

It all starts on Friday afternoon. Some people are wearing their own costumes, others I gather work somewhere at the event—just like me! Then, Saturday is the busiest day, with all the costumes and laughing, and people saying hello. There's hugging, too. I like the hugging.

Sunday is a mixed bag. It's more relaxed on Sunday, but people tend to spend less time in my room. They say it smells, but it's their smell, not mine.

I enjoy seeing all the different types of people who visit over the weekend; I could watch them forever. Some are young and some are older. Some are larger, and some much smaller. Many move on legs, and others wheels. They have high voices, and low voices, and some don't say anything at all. They have eyes of every color, eyes in slightly different places, and sometimes just one eye. They can have big hair, short hair, covered hair, hair that even comes off, or no hair at all. Some are moms and some are friends and some are more than that! Yes! I've seen them kissing!

I like to read their funny shirts. I wish I could tell them how funny some are. And how ironic! I want to say, "Master of Sarcasm. *Suuure* you are."

The smallest children have the hardest time. They can't always see me, and I can't see them. But then someone lifts them up and they smile. Just like Sheila lifted me up. So I think I know how that feels.

Some of the costumes I like more than others. Some of the groups dress all the same, wearing small skirts. I like it better when they look different. And when they picked their costume themselves. I can always tell when they picked it themselves.

I really like Wonder Woman. I've heard in real life, she tells the truth and stops bullets and saves the world. And people dress up like her with big shields. And when they lift that shield, they look like they're stopping bullets too.

I just don't understand why anyone would want to start bullets in the first place. I guess that's why we need Wonder Woman.

Of all the costumes, the homemade ones are the best. People mutter at me, saying their costumes are not the best, but they're wrong. Every moment of sewing, painting, and designing that goes into a homemade costume is another moment of art injected into the world. I suspect my sink thinks that's a little much. I don't. I think it's correct.

People use me for pictures. Can you believe it? I'm on the internet! They tilt and hold their phones, and *snap!* "Posted!" they giggle. Not everyone seems so happy about this. Sometimes people scowl and duck out of the way. Then they go back to putting on their makeup.

Makeup is a funny thing. It can bring a costume to life, but it hides the person beneath. That's fine—as long as they like the person beneath. But I hear people telling their friends how bad they look, as they cover themselves up. "No!" I want to shout. They don't look bad. No one looks bad.

I'm happy to be a mirror, but by myself, I'm a flat sheet of glass. No color, no texture, no variation. People—they are amazing. They're made in every shape and curve and bump and shade. And when I see them, I can be those things too. Bad? No. You never look bad.

I think you're super.

I think you're perfect.

If I could talk, I'd tell each child and woman and person who comes into this room how much I love to see them. I'd tell them how much I love their colors, their shapes, and most of all, their smiles.

Next time you're here, give me a smile and a wink.

Ha! I tricked you. You'll be smiling and winking at you, too.

Personally, I think you deserve it.

++

Atthis Arts is an independent publisher out of Detroit, Michigan. We believe in the artistic voice of the author being at the core of our projects. We also believe in amplifying creative voices, including those traditionally marginalized. We are proud of and stand by our commitment to diversity and inclusion. Our anthologies are designed to be safe for a diverse reader base—our submission guidelines specifically prohibit harmful messaging toward culture, background, religion, ethic, gender, orientation, attraction, race, ethnicity, ability, or body.

Copyright Acknowledgements